ENDORSEMENTS

Doris Grace is an artist who paints a personal portrait of life the way she recalls it. Using a palette of words she fills the canvas of her recollection with colorful images, characters and stories that picture a much simpler time. As one who also tells stories on paper, I celebrate her ability to welcome the reader into her world. As her name suggests, Doris provides us with a work of art that is framed with reality and grace.

Greg Asimakoupoulos, pastor, newspaper columnist and freelance writer, Mercer Island, WA

In this charming, heart-warming memoir, Doris Grace looks back with fondness and gratitude on her upbringing in the beautiful Missouri Ozarks at a time when children ran barefoot through the fields and explored caves on their own, largely unbothered by the economic troubles that worried their parents in that Depression era. Her evocative descriptions and amusing anecdotes bring to life the freedom and innocence of that place and time, re-creating a world that is no more. The author's warm, conversational style will draw you into her life and times and keep you reading to the end.

Dawn Thurston, author of *Breathe Life Into Your Life Story: How to Write a Story People Will Want to Read*, published by Signature Books, 2007

Doris Grace's memoir transports the reader to the 1930's to a community in the Missouri Ozarks that was suspended in time. In her mind she spent her early childhood "in the most beautiful place on earth." With her heart and mind bolstered by images of beauty and truth, Doris' plain-spoken memoir tells a story of a life lived with courage, energy and faith that came out of a foundation of all that is best in rural Americana.

Hugh Steven, Author-at-large, Wycliffe Bible Translators, Retired.

Doris Grace's memoir describes her full life that began in the Ozarks of Missouri. Her writing has a lyrical sound, tinged with "Missouri-ese." And her early childhood memories display her native intelligence. The charming songs that her parents sang to her are a precursor to her interest in music that led to her performance at Carnegie Hall. Her story reveals her love of her family, her God and her music. It is a grand legacy to her family.

Vernagene Vogelzang, Author, former columnist the The Modesto Bee, McClatchy Newspapers

God brought into my life Doris Grace and her husband Dick, who took care of me and my family when we landed in the USA from India for studies at Fuller Theological Seminary. Since then, for many years, their home has become not only my home when I visit California, but the home of countless men and women of God from other parts of the world.

Robert Cunville, Associate Evangelist, Billy Graham Evangelistic Association

How Sweet the Sound

A Memoir

Doris J. Grace

iUniverse

HOW SWEET THE SOUND
A MEMOIR

iUniverse books may be ordered through booksellers or by contacting:

iUniverse
1663 Liberty Drive
Bloomington, IN 47403
www.iuniverse.com
844-349-9409

Because of the dynamic nature of the Internet, any web addresses or links contained in this book may have changed since publication and may no longer be valid. The views expressed in this work are solely those of the author and do not necessarily reflect the views of the publisher, and the publisher hereby disclaims any responsibility for them.

Any people depicted in stock imagery provided by Getty Images are models, and such images are being used for illustrative purposes only. Certain stock imagery © Getty Images.

ISBN: 978-1-4401-8849-7 (sc)
ISBN: 978-1-4401-8851-0 (hc)
ISBN: 978-1-4401-8850-3 (e)

Printed in the United States of America

iUniverse rev. date: 10/25/2022

* INTRODUCTION *

Memory is selective, and I have not attempted to be encyclopedic, but have found that the main focus of my memoir is on my earlier years in the Missouri Ozarks. These years were so different than those lived in the 21st Century. We lived in a country home without running water or indoor plumbing and, in my earlier years, no heat except from the kitchen wood-burning cookstove. But I believe it was a carefree life for a child and, even though there were dangers such as getting lost in the woods, getting bit by snakes, or becoming very ill without proper medical care, I had intelligent parents who made good choices for us. My children, Susan, Debra and Thomas, loved to hear stories of my childhood, and I hope that my three grandchildren, Grayson, Janna and Jackson, will also enjoy reading about them. I dedicate this memoir to them.

Memory also includes stories by others in my family, particularly my parents, and some things are repeated from their reminiscences. They communicated by writing letters, telling stories and by telephone. Communication is different these days as we send e-mails back and forth to family. But e-mail letters are seldom saved, and there is a loss because of that.

I have chosen the title of this memoir from the internationally-known hymn *Amazing Grace, How Sweet the Sound*. I think it describes my love of music, the name Grace fortunately acquired upon marriage, and my faith, saved by the loving grace of God.

ACKNOWLEDGMENTS

This book is all about family. My parents, my grandparents, my aunts and uncles, all had a primary part in my life. The larger Randel and Lewis families came together regularly just to enjoy one another. When Grandma Lewis was living with Mom and Dad in Riverside, California, the local Lewis clan would arrive at their house on Sunday afternoons, still dressed in their Sunday best, to sit in a big circle and visit. Dad often made a freezer of home-made ice cream to share.

My brother Willie and my sister Emily have been close to me. Willie and I ran and played in the woods and fields of rural Missouri when we were children. He was my playmate and my protector. My sister Emily and I have been the best and most intimate friends as well, particularly during the years when our mother was suffering her protracted bout with senile dementia. We spent at least one day a week together, in the beginning including Mom, of course, but when she went into a care facility, we visited her there but spent the day at lunch and perhaps shopping. On occasion Willie and Verna joined us for lunch, driving from El Cajon, about a two hour trip.

Our three children, Susan, Debra and Thomas, have been the ideal family. I could not have asked for a closer and dearer family. And now, with three grandchildren, Grayson, Janna and Jackson, I am deeply blessed.

We have friends everywhere over the world but probably our closest friends have been couples we met at Berkeley First Presbyterian Church, Garden Grove First Presbyterian and Trinity Presbyterian, Santa Ana. We count many of them as close as family. And in reality, they are our heavenly family.

Thanks to Hugh Steven who edited this memoir. I am grateful to him for his professionalism and interest in giving the manuscript his close attention. His years as a writer of more than forty books gives him the expertise needed to turn out a clean and concise volume.

Thanks also to Dawn Thurston, my writing teacher. She continuously offers new and innovative ideas to make books and stories interesting to read.

I reserve this last paragraph for my dear Dick. As a skinny kid in rural Missouri, I never dreamed that because of him I would travel the world. We have counted over seventy countries visited over twenty-five years of travel. He is loving and considerate, a great Dad and the best husband. Thank you, Dick, for seeing me as a kid of sixteen and deciding that I would be yours.

HOW SWEET THE SOUND

A Memoir By

Doris J. Grace

"We all come from the past, and children ought to know what it was that went into their making, to know that life is a braided cord of humanity stretching up from time long gone."

Russell Baker, Growing Up

C * H * A * P * T * E * R

* 1 *

CHILDHOOD IN THE OZARKS

As a child, thick hardwood forests of the Ozark Mountains enclosed me in a cocoon of protection from the worries and troubles of the world. It was a carefree time, a time to roam the hills and valleys, wade the creeks, climb trees and jump in my uncle's haymow.

In the summer my older brother Wilton and I went barefoot. We played, fought, and explored our world with freedom and abandon. We made up games and carried out our own traditions all four seasons of the year. When late spring arrived and we were finally allowed to go barefoot, we had an annual ritual of running fifty yards down the gravel driveway barefoot to the front gate. Wilton, always superior, shouted, "Bet I can beat you." But never to give in by default just because I was younger and smaller, I spurted out as fast my legs would carry me, enduring the pain of gravel tearing into my tender, winter-softened feet. I always lost.

I was a skinny kid of average height with light brown wavy hair and green eyes, the second child of my father and mother, Elmer Folk Randel and Edna Mae Lewis, descendants of early Americans. Our ancestors are a duke's mixture of English, German, Scots-Irish and Welsh with a tad of Choctaw Native American Indian thrown in. More than a few were Revolutionary War soldiers and all four of my great-grandfathers were in the Civil War.

For the first few years of my life we were a close-knit family of four. Then, when I was eight years old and my brother eleven, my sweet baby sister arrived. Baby Emily replaced my dolls as a plaything and in my mind I became a miniature surrogate mother.

Doris and Baby Emily

In 1932, the year I was born, the country was still in the midst of the Great Depression and geo-political events in Europe and Asia would soon have dire consequence for the world. Herbert Hoover was president that year and the first woman in history was elected to Congress. But the international news was grim and the specter of World War II would deeply affect all young people of my generation.

Tucked away from civilization in Ripley County, Missouri, in the foothills of the Ozark Mountains, down a spine-like ridge on a narrow dirt road, past Aunt Mary's house and the Old Lewis Cemetery, and across the cave spring branch, rests the foundation of my little white house of childhood. The house itself burned in the 1940s and another structure was built on the native rock foundation.

It is across the field from the Lewis Cave, once a local tourist attraction that belongs to my mother's Lewis family. The Cave is no longer open to the public but family members may enjoy exploring it when they visit the family roots. A few years after my husband Dick and I were married I took him to the Big Barren community in Ripley County for the first time. With a wry smile he asked, "How did you *ever* find your way out of here?"

In my mind and heart, Ripley County is among the most beautiful places on earth. It rests just north of the Arkansas state line and is in the eastern part of the state, in the foothills of the Ozarks. In summertime it's a tourist mecca, inviting fishermen, boaters, swimmers, hikers and nature lovers to come and visit. In springtime the thick woods are filled with redbud and dogwood trees in riotous bloom of red and white, a stark contrast to the bare branches of the other deciduous trees, not yet leafed-out. In the fall the black walnut, oak, hickory, sycamore, elm and maple trees are smeared with a color palette of yellow, red, orange, and all shades in between. Evergreen cedar and pine trees are here also and they offer a contrast to the bouquet. The Ozark Mountains here are not as high as the peaks to the west and south of Ripley County. It is believed that these venerable hills are among the most ancient on earth and are rounded at top, covered with beauteous hardwood and evergreen forests.

Heaven help you if a tornado hits in the locality of my Ozarks. By the time you see it coming, twisting and blowing over the nearest hills, it would be too late to take cover. On stormy days we learned to carefully watch cloud formations, looking for danger. Early one morning when I was about nine, my Mom rousted Wilton and me out of bed, quickly grabbed baby Emily from her crib and said, "Run for the cave, tornado coming." As we ran down the driveway towards safety, Dad came running down the field, swinging his milk bucket. He had been out to milk the cow and decided it was too dangerous to delay a minute. He often thought Mom was too quick to worry about potential tornados, but this particular morning he too saw the danger. A tornado didn't hit us that morning, but did, indeed, touch down a few miles away, causing extensive damage.

In the springtime, creeks and rivers are filled to overflow and rivulets tumble down from high places. This part of the State of Missouri rests on a limestone base and water filters down into and through the cracks in the limestone to produce clear pure waters in artesian wells and springs. Big Spring, a Missouri State Park about ten miles from my childhood home, produces an unbelievable amount of pure water that flows into the Current River—the source of delight for water sports lovers.[1]

There are no freeways to take you to Ripley County, and you cannot fly there or take the train or a bus. In years past, one could actually take the train to Doniphan, the county seat, but it has long ago ceased to run. In the Doniphan Museum there is a large picture of army troops, recruited from the County, all dressed in their uniforms and waiting on the train platform for the train to take them to the battlefields of World War I. My Uncle Bob Randel was one of them. Today, the mode of transportation to Ripley County is your own vehicle.

When my eighty-five year old Aunt Zelma visited me a few years ago, and was planning her trip home to Doniphan, she intended to take a plane from California to St. Louis and a bus to Poplar Bluff, about thirty miles from Doniphan. "But Aunt Zelma," I asked, "how will you get to Doniphan from there?"

"No problem," she said, "I'll just go over to Wal-Mart and stand outside until I see someone from Doniphan. They'll take me." And that is exactly what happened.

If you asked me to draw a map of my Big Barren community, I would locate it in the northwest quadrant of the county. In the local dialect it's called "Big Barn." My map would include the whole Mark Twain National Forest, the creeks, rivers and country roads, but only

---

[1]   Located near Van Buren, Missouri in the Ozarks, Big Spring is the largest spring in the state, and one of the largest in the world. On an average day, some 278 million gallons of water gush forth from subterranean passages, swelling the nearby Current River. Experiments in which harmless dye is placed into the ground have shown that water travels from as far as 45 miles away through underground passages before coming to the surface at Big Spring.
Like all Ozark springs, Big Spring is busy dissolving away the walls of its underground passages. One researcher estimated that about 175 tons of calcium carbonate rock are carried away in solution by Big Spring's water every day! Over the course of a year, this is enough rock to produce a cavern thirty feet wide by fifty feet wide and one mile in length. http://en.wikipedia.org/wiki/Big_Spring_(Missouri)

isolated farms and farmhouses. It would include the little one-room schoolhouse I attended for my first seven years of education.

At present, these little schools have been closed and the children are all bussed to Lone Star School, near Doniphan. Van Buren is the closest town to my community, about fifteen miles away, and Doniphan, the county seat of Ripley County, is almost thirty miles away. We always went to Doniphan for supplies and when I speak of "town," I mean *that* community of about 1,800 people. In the 1930s and 1940s, Doniphan, its main street lined with century-old wooden buildings, swelled to almost twice its size on Saturdays when farmers came to trade farm produce for necessary staples.

Wild creatures roam these woods, deer, turkeys, red foxes, bobcats, rabbits, squirrels, raccoons and opossum (locally known as 'coon and 'possum). There are also numerous species of snakes, both poisonous and nonpoisonous. As a child, I was taught to never take a step without looking where I was going during the warm months of the year, where in the thick underbrush a snake could lie coiled and ready to strike.

But the birds! Oh, how melodious and splendid are the songbirds of the Ozarks; bobwhite, cardinals, bluejays, woodpeckers, martins, mockingbirds. On a visit back home after many years, I simply could not go to sleep for listening to the musical mating call of "whip-por-will, whip-por-will" in the night, only to be answered by a neighboring call from further away.

I must mention the wonderful flowering shrubs in the springtime. Lilacs were my favorite; purple and white, they have the most marvelous aroma. My mother grew gladiolas, hollyhocks, tiger lilies and other annuals and we often cut armfuls of these flowers to take to the Lewis Cemetery to decorate the family graves.

Why, you might ask, do I consider my real home to be in the Ozarks when I left at age twelve and have never lived there again. I have searched my heart and pondered this dilemma many times over. Roots—what does that mean? As young parents my husband and I took our three children to visit the Missouri Ozarks. In the deepest sense of the word I had come home, even though I had lived in three other places since leaving. Why was that? At the time I could not really understand or, more particularly, really articulate my feelings. It seemed like a certain pull from the landscape; affecting me some place deep in my body. It wasn't my head or my heart; it was someplace new to me that I couldn't seem to locate at first, or give it a name. It was a deep pull, like a feeling of gravity. I have recently read an opinion that genes, or DNA, have the ability to store ancestral memories. And these can survive for hundreds of years.[2] Perhaps that is the answer.

~ ~ ~ ~

Early Memories

My very first memory comes from the time we lived with Granddad and Grandma Lewis in their old log house on the hill. Isn't it strange how some memories come to the surface after having been buried for so many years? In thinking about my Grandma and Granddad's log house, I remembered being placed in my baby buggy outside the kitchen door for a nap under a big tree. It was believed that the fresh air was beneficial to the health of little ones. I vaguely remember being afraid to be out there alone, but mother murmured soothing words, saying something like, "Doris Jane, go to sleep now in your buggy. It is good and healthy for you to get some good fresh air while you're sleeping." I remember watching the leaves on the tree flutter in the breeze as I dozed off to sleep.

Another profound memory occurred some months later, when I was toddling around. Mom took me to our new house that was under construction. We went into the basement to look at progress being made and while Mom was distracted, I crawled up the stairs to see what was up there. However, when I arrived at the top, I could see that the floor was not in place. There were only floor joists with lots of space in between. Terribly frightened, I began to cry which alerted Mom who dashed up the steps and rescue me. These earliest memories were etched into my memory, possibly through fear.

Another early, vague memory is of waking up early in the crib in my parents' bedroom and purposefully making enough noise so that Mom would come and get me. She was so very glad to greet me and I felt special to her. Even though I don't ever remember Mom rocking

---

[2]   Feiler, Bruce, *Walking The Bible, 2005, p.410*

me or cuddling me, I remember two sad songs that she sang when she was getting me to sleep; perhaps I was rocked then:

LITTLE FERNS

Oh, what shall we do the long winter through?
The baby ferns cried when the mother fern died.
The wind whistled bleak and the woodland was drear,
And on each baby cheek there glistened a tear.

Tucked under the snow in their little white hoods,
These tiny white things with their little green wings.
They fell in a heap where the baby ferns lay
And went right to sleep that bleak stormy day.

They slept sound and snug under snow and cold rain
The baby ferns dreamed of warm days to come.
Till one day in spring when the bob-o-link sings
They will open their eyes to the bluest of skies.

KITTY

Oh kitty, my little grey kitty,
I've hunted the house all around.
I've looked in the cradle and under the table
But nowhere could kitty be found.

I took my hook and went to the brook
To see if my kitty was there
And when I found my kitty was drowned
Why then I gave up in despair.

～ ～ ～

VACATION TO THE WEST:

Dad always had a fascination for the western part of our country. He and Mom had driven an old Chevrolet coupe to Colorado on their honeymoon. Dad often reminisced about living in the West someday.

When I was not quite four years old, Dad and Mom took Wilton and me, along with Uncle Nace and his girlfriend, Wilma Buffington, on a motor trip west. We were gone two weeks and I have only a few memories of this, my first big excursion away from home.

Thinking back now, we must have been quite crowded in the car with four adults and two kids. No seat belts in those days of course. I remember that we went to see the Painted Desert, Petrified Forest and Grand Canyon. Driving across the red-dirt deserts, the burning blue sky seemed to stretch forever on each side of the highway. When I saw the native plants of the desert and the many varieties of cactus, ocotillo bush, yucca—it was like entering another world. I was fascinated with the jackrabbits, leaping across the road in front of the car. Their big ears made them so different from the wild bunnies in the woods of Missouri. We then went north to Yellowstone National Park and Pikes Peak before starting home. I remember Dad's great love of the beautiful, mountainous scenery with deep, green forests and waterfalls spilling millions of gallons of water down high cliffs. I remember eating bologna sandwiches in the car and having the bread get dry and hard before the sandwich was consumed. It was such a phenomenon to me, having always lived in a humid climate. In my child's mind, it seemed we had been gone from home forever. As we approached our home community, I tapped Dad on his shoulder and said, "Daddy, will you stop the car up the road from Grandma's house and let me walk down the road to her house to see if she recognizes me?"

Elmer and Edna Randel

I compared almost any man I ever knew to Dad to see if he measured up. As children, standing on a bluff over a deep pond, Wilton and I once philosophized:

"Bet Uncle Lee couldn't swim across that deep pond."

"Bet God couldn't swim across that deep pond."

"Heck, that's nothing. I'll bet even Dad couldn't swim across it."

He was a man whose heart was stitched together with steel wire. Dad was strong, yet tender, a man of integrity and good character and a leader in the community. Of average height, about five feet ten, with a slender build, his face was sharp carved with large nose, elongated ears and high forehead. Light brown hair and bright blue eyes perhaps betrayed his Anglo-Saxon heritage. He normally wore bib overalls for every day, but if he planned to drive to town his outfit for the day would be khaki pants and long-sleeved shirt, open at the neck.

He served on the local school board and occasionally acted as parole officer to local folks who had been in trouble with the law, usually for cutting timber on government land, locally called "grandmawing."

He loved music and poetry and sang dozens of songs and recited poetry he learned as a child. Here's a song I've never seen in print, but we children heard Dad sing it many times:

ARAWANNA

'Mid the wild and wooly prairies lived an Indian maid,
Arawanna, queen of fairies and her tribe of braves.
Each night came an Irish laddie-buck with a wedding ring,
He would sit outside her tent and with his bagpipe loudly sing:

Refrain:
Arawanna, on my honor, I'll take care of you,
I'll be kind and true.
We can love and bill and coo
In a wigwam built of shamrock green
We'll make those red men smile,
With Mrs. Barney, heap much Carney
From Killarney's Isle.

While the moon shone down upon them, Arawanna cried:
Some great race must call you Big Chief
Then I'll be your bride.
Sure that's easy whispered Barney with a smiling face,

All my family were great runners and the first in every race.

Dad was a rhythm-maker, drumming on any surface available, tapping out rhythms with his fingers, making unique sounds with his hands while clapping and even slapping his legs in rhythm. He continued this rhythm-making until the day he died, even after his voice was damaged from a stroke and he could no longer sing. On the day of his death, he was pecking a rhythm on the side rails of his hospital bed.

I never, ever felt unloved, uncared for or uneasy about my future, but it only came as a nuance in Dad's character. In the 1930s it just wasn't the custom for people to hug and kiss one another. Parenthetically, I remember seeing a cousin greet her father with only a handshake after a separation of many months. It would have been most unusual for Dad to express himself with a hug, even among family members.

Dad was born to Lewis Austin Randel and Ida Hufstedler, while they lived on a farm a few miles northwest of Doniphan, Missouri, the seventh child of the family. As a young lad, Dad was expected to carry his load of heavy farm work, such as plowing, milking and chopping wood.

When he was a boy of thirteen tragedy struck Elmer's family. His mother Ida contracted tuberculosis and died at the age of forty-one, leaving a family of eight children, the youngest of whom was not quite two years old. Five children had previously either died at birth or, in the case of little Claude Casey, died at age six. Austin was so shocked and devastated he was unable to properly care for the family's personal needs in addition to the necessary farm work. He was so numbed by grief he could not offer emotional support for his children.

Dad had only one memory of his father praising him and that was only by overhearing a chance conversation. After Dad and his brother Nace went to bed one night, they overheard their father telling an adult in the kitchen, "Those boys did a real good job of plowing today." How sad for my father, probably starved for affection, growing up with only one instance of praise from his father and, on top of that, losing his mother.

The family rallied around and tried valiantly to take care of household chores and cooking. My Uncle Nace was a boy of eleven and it became his job to cut the hair of his siblings. Aunt Marie was a little tyke of four with long blond curls and, since they didn't know how to care for her hair, Uncle Nace just cut off all the curls to make her resemble a sad little boy. Two older sisters, Ollye and Carolyn "Cad" did the cooking and tried to assume the mothering.

In warm weather, after supper when the chores were done, it was the custom for the family to sit on the front porch, telling stories, sometimes singing, and listening to the whip-por-wills and owls hooting in the trees. Dad and other youngsters would sit on the porch floor. Sleepy from the long day, Dad would sometimes curl up on the cold, hard boards and fall asleep. Awaking in the small hours of the night, with the rest of the family already gone to bed, he knew he had to wash his feet before climbing upstairs to bed. That was one of the rules.

Austin stumbled through his days in a fog of despair and the family reflected this sadness. These sad years surely marked my Dad with grief. Although he and my Mom most certainly loved one another, his ability to make himself totally vulnerable and love others was compromised.

Dad's educational career got off to a rocky start. On the first day of school when he was six and due to begin his education, he hid under the house and refused to come out. One of the older siblings had to crawl under there to retrieve him and start him down the hill and across the field to Lone Star School.

As a teenager, Dad walked about three or four miles to town to attend high school. Since he was not a resident of the city, there was a small tuition. Austin sold a young heifer to pay the tuition for Dad's freshman year and managed to come up with the required money for the next two years, but when Dad would have been a senior, there was absolutely no way he could find the needed money. So Dad didn't start school. A week or two after the fall term began, he was in town on an errand when the President of the Bank, Pope Whitwell, came charging out the front door of the bank. "Elmer," he called, "Come over here."

Dad obediently crossed the street.

"Why aren't you in school?"

Hanging his head, Dad mumbled, "There is no money for tuition."

Mr. Whitwell took him by the arm. "Come on in the bank and we'll arrange a loan." So with no collateral, this kind man loaned Dad enough money to finish high school.

Back in the nineteen twenties in that part of the country, it was considered quite an accomplishment to get a high school diploma. Many of the rural boys and girls left school after the eighth grade. Dad was understandably proud that he got his diploma and felt he was ready to go out into the world. Like many of his generation, he believed a high school education was a sufficient formal education for us children. The result was a struggle of wills to obtain higher education in the mid-twentieth century.

My father had seen the continual hard, unremitting labor of a farmer and, after he graduated, he vowed never to follow in the footsteps of his father and grandfather before him. Perhaps as an avenue of escape, he took the same route lots of other local high school graduates of both sexes took by sitting for the Missouri State teachers' examination. He passed this difficult exam, and to pay back his bank loan, he taught eight grades at one of the rural one-room schools in Ripley County for a year. But teaching didn't suit his fancy either—he wasn't to find his life's work as a scholar and teacher. Some of his older siblings had moved to St. Louis to find work and so Dad joined them, living with his brother and sister-in-law, Uncle Bob and Aunt Frieda Randel. He got a job at General Motors and was trained to tend the large storage batteries in the factory.

C * H * A * P * T * E * R

* 3 *

By the time my mother was born to James Hale and Abbie May Lewis, they were likely to have been weary from having so many children—at least I would guess that was true of Grandma. Similarly, my Aunt Mayme Lewis once lamented, "I had so many children I couldn't look another one in the face, and then I had twins."

There were eight older siblings when Mom was born in 1907 in their little log house on a hill in the thick woods, just north of the Lewis Cave.

Lewis Log House

When she and her two younger sisters came along, several of the older children had already left home, so the younger children were assigned regular chores as soon as they were old enough to work. Mom was a pretty child although she felt inferior to her older sister Velda.

When visitors came, and in Edna's presence complimented Velda for her beautiful dark curls, Edna claimed the visitor would then look at her and say nothing. Mom was petite, only five feet tall at maturity and always slender. She also had dark curls, complimented by deep amber eyes, possibly reflecting her Welsh heritage. She possessed a placid and loving personality, undergirded with strength and innate optimism.

She was a strong advocate when it came to offering us children opportunities to excel. Knowing how much I loved music, she saw to it that when I reached my teen years in Michigan I received both piano and vocal lessons.

She and Dad made a good pair, but Dad's sometimes rigid decisions, coupled with his strict head-of-the-family stance, sometimes caused Mom to be a little devious and do end runs around Dad's decisions. On occasion she might say, "Now we won't need to tell your father about this."

When Mom went to high school in Doniphan, she moved from the Big Barren Community and boarded with her older brother and his wife, Gus and Bertha Lewis. She and Dad met at school and were soon attracted to one another. It was a custom of Dad's cousin, Horace Hufstedler, to take his friends for drives in the county on Sunday afternoons in his father's roadster. My mother and father were two of his regular Sunday passengers. Mom was elated one day at school when Dad said, "Edna, when we take rides on Sunday with Horace, I would like it understood that you are with me." Mom had already fallen for him so that was music to her ears. So they became a pair, devoted to one another. They were eventually married for sixty-two years until Dad's death in 1991.

After high school and before she and Dad were married, Edna taught elementary school for a couple of years in rural Ripley County in typical one room school houses, where she taught grades one through eight. She told of riding a horse to her school, and often was so tired after a day of teaching, would lay the reins across the horse's neck and say, "Home, Snappy." The old mare knew the way. In later years, she was my seventh grade teacher, returning to Big Barren School during World War II when there was a scarcity of teachers caused by younger women leaving traditional occupations to work in war factories and joining the armed forces as WACs or nurses.

After a couple of years teaching, Mom left Ripley County and went to St. Louis to be near Elmer. She got a job and boarded with her Aunt Ada Ertle. Aunt Ada was a strict disciplinarian and didn't believe Edna when she was told she had eloped.

Edna Lewis as a Teenager

They planned the elopement in May of 1929. Mom bought a beautiful dress for the occasion. It was a salmon-colored, dropped waist chiffon dress, with two rows of ruffles near the hem, flapper style. Dressed and waiting on the morning of the elopement, she remembered looking out the front window of Aunt Ada's house and, when she saw Elmer coming up the walk to get her, all dressed in suit and tie, thought, *He's the handsomest man I've ever seen.*

They drove across the Missouri River to St. Charles, Missouri and were married before a Justice of the Peace with only one witness, the Justice's wife. For years afterward, Mom was concerned that because they didn't have two witnesses their marriage wasn't completely legal.

After the ceremony the newly married couple returned to Aunt Ada's, anxious to reveal their marvelous news. Aunt Ada, however, was suspicious. She turned to her son Leslie Ertle and commanded him, "Leslie, I want you to go over to St. Charles to this Justice of the Peace to see if Edna has actually run off and got married."

My brother Wilton Lewis Randel was born not long after the stock market crash in December of that year. For awhile Dad retained his job at Chevrolet, but as the months and years passed, the country sunk further into the Great Depression. Because there no money except for meat and potatoes, I was born at home on July 8, 1932. When the birth seemed imminent, they called the doctor. After he arrived he said, "Elmer, I want you to go down to the drugstore and buy some ether," thus getting him out of the house for the imminent birth. Sure enough, I chose to arrive before Dad returned to the house.

Mom used to tell me, "You have never caused me any trouble; even your birth was easy." So all was well and my mother and father were elated to have a little son and a baby daughter. I was born in a tiny little house on Betty Lee Avenue in the St. John district of St. Louis. The little cottage still stands in the neighborhood where Aunt Marie Jennings and Uncle Woodrow Randel, Dad's sister and brother, had homes.

Doris's Birthplace

Six months later, as the Great Depression closed in my Dad lost his job. We located back south to Ripley County where Mother's parents granted us a little plot of land on the Lewis farm. Two new houses were planned, a new one for Grandma and Granddad Lewis and one for us. In a letter to a nephew in Texas, Granddad wrote, "We are moving off the hill, it's harder for us old folks to get up and down the steep path."

Our little family of four moved into the log house with Granddad and Grandma until both new houses could be finished. My Uncle Chester Lewis, a master carpenter, came from St. Louis to do the building and Dad happily joined him to learn the skills. They removed rock from the Lewis Farm for the foundations and had the timber chopped down and taken to the mill to plane into lumber.

~ ~ ~ ~

During our years in the 1930s and early 1940s, Dad was troubled from time to time with what he called *la grippe*, which was respiratory illness or chronic bronchitis. It became clear to Mom she would need to learn how to drive our 1941 Ford pick-up to help him. Dad taught her and she drove up and down the dirt roads in our Big Barren community before gathering enough courage to drive to town. The stick shift was her bane; she never really conquered the mystery of when to shift to a lower gear.

One incidence stands out in family memory. It was time to take a load of hogs to market and Dad was down with *la grippe*. I don't remember how the hogs got loaded into the truck bed of our pick-up, but it became Mom's duty to drive those hogs to Doniphan to market.

The big danger in all of this was the church-house hill, a steep, rutted dirt road that began its ascent at the church and climbed upwards a good quarter mile to the larger and better-maintained "C" Road on top of the ridge. Mom had other passengers that day, a couple of local men riding to town on a wooden board suspended above the hogs. They paid twenty-five cents each for the ride.

"Edna," my Dad instructed, "You will need to shift down on the hill to make it to the top."

"I don't know how to shift on a hill," worried Mom. "What if the truck starts rolling backwards when I push in the clutch?"

Dad's answer remains lost in my memory except for something about double-clutching. Mom got behind the wheel and valiantly headed out. She secretly had a plan: Make a fast, running start up the hill on that narrow and rutted dirt road and labor upwards to the C Road without shifting. The story became a local legend of how Mom did this very thing with gritted teeth, lurching up that hill like a demon possessed, and as the truck climbed slower and slower, made it over the top by sheer will power. To this day I do not understand why one of those neighbor men didn't drive. Perhaps they didn't know how.

Mom was always a white-knuckle driver and, when we moved to Michigan in 1944 to urban living, she never drove again. However, the year she taught school at Big Barren, she drove the pick-up every morning. When the creek was flooding and the road impassable, she walked "over the hill" to school with Wilton and me.

Beginning with that year of teaching, she became a career woman and never returned to being a full-time homemaker. When we moved to Michigan, Mom went to work in a war plant, working in the tool shed six and seven days a week, checking out various and sundry tools to the workers on the assembly lines.

When the war was over, she worked for the State of Michigan Unemployment Association, learning to be a crackerjack operator of a comptometer machine—an early calculator—and when we moved to California she worked for the Burpee Seed Company and the U.S. Farm Bureau in Riverside. She then was hired by Security Title Insurance Company as a bookkeeper and, by the time she retired, was head of her department of thirty-five people.

At home after her professional years, she kept busy with her gift of hand-crafted quilting, making beautiful heirlooms for each of her ten grandchildren. She put in a garden each spring in a vacant field behind the back wall of their home, and gave away fresh vegetables to family, neighbors and friends. One summer in her late seventies she canned eighty quarts of home grown tomatoes.

Mom had a quiet, deep faith in the Lord Jesus. Her serene and placid personality reflected this faith. But she had a fierce strength when it came to her three children. She was our first advocate and went about finding ways to help us be upstanding and responsible citizens.

When she was about eighty and still able-bodied, her mind was attacked by senile dementia. The dementia moved slowly but methodically, destroying her mind so that towards the end she went to weddings and funerals that had taken place in her younger years. On other days she cooked and canned and hosted family dinners, moving across time and traveling among the lost decades with speed and ease. I first noticed something awry one day when I took her to shop for new shoes.

"What is your shoe size?" inquired the clerk.

"Size six," she said confidently.

Mom had worn size eight for several years, but in her younger years, size six was her shoe size. A warning bell rang in my mind. Was something happening to Mom? A month or two later, visiting her doctor, he gave her one of those oral quizzes that medical personnel use to determine potential problems. She failed, giving wrong answers to ordinary questions such as "What year is this?" "Who is president?"

"Abraham Lincoln," retorted Mom, attempting levity as a solution.

For a time we, her family, attempted to set her straight. Perhaps what she needed was a good explanation for things she had temporarily forgotten. It was such a foolish, innocent idea, but this was our intelligent, school teacher Mom. Other people can become frail and break, but not parents. However, reality eventually settled in and I stopped trying to wrest her back to what I considered the real world and went along with her fantastic swoops into the past. Visiting her at her board and care home in her last years, she would smile her sweet smile and say, "My sweetie is coming for me today. He's going to take me home." But her sweetie, my Dad, whose name she couldn't articulate anymore, had been dead for years. She lived for ninety-eight years and ninety-eight days.

C * H * A * P * T * E * R

* 4 *

When I was eight and Wilton was eleven, we had an addition to the family, little Emily Imogene arrived on December 23, 1940. Mom's favorite story regarding the labor and birth is that Dad, in his excitement to get her to town to the hospital, forgot to fill the truck with gas. When they were about ten or fifteen miles out of town he had to leave her on a grassy bank at the side of the road and go for fuel. Thankfully for all, Emily didn't arrive until after he retrieved Mom from the bank and they made it safely to the hospital.

Despite the predictions of neighbors and relatives, I do not remember being jealous of Emily. Perhaps the age difference between us made me feel more maternal towards her. She was always our little pet and I imagine that we all spoiled her thoroughly. We left country living for Michigan when she was three, so there aren't many memories of country life with her in the picture.

I do remember one incident, however, that is quite vivid. It was spring and, as usual, the creeks were flooding. We set out on a Sunday morning for Cliff and Clarice Moore's house near Bennett for Sunday dinner. I was excited because Mary Ellen Moore was my best friend and second cousin and I got to play with her all too seldom. Clarice and Mom were first cousins, her father Ernest Glore and Mom's mother, Abbie Glore Lewis, were brother and sister. When we arrived at the road below the schoolhouse where we had to ford the creek, it was rising rapidly and becoming dangerous to cross. But Dad decided to try. Sure enough, half way across, the engine stalled and Dad couldn't get it started. It was raining hard and the creek was rising fast. Dad knew he had to act fast.

"Edna," he said, "I am going to wade out and go over to Raymond Lewis' house and get him to bring his team of mules to pull us out. You take the kids, wade out of the creek and up the side of the hill to the Mills' house."

Time was of the essence, because the raging creek could soon wash the truck off the road and wreck it on the rocks. So Dad waded out and went to get help from Raymond Lewis, who lived nearby. Mom took us kids up the bank where we knocked at the door of Mr. and Mrs. Mills, an elderly couple. They, of course, invited us in, but didn't offer us anything to eat. I remember sitting in their living room for what seemed like hours, listening to an old grandfather clock go "tick-tock, tick-tock" in the silence, and thinking I was starving to death. *Why couldn't they just offer us some soda crackers?* I thought, as my stomach growled in protest.

After what seemed like forever, Dad came to the house. "Well, the truck has been pulled out of the creek. However, I can't drive it because the creeks have risen so high they are not passable. So we will have to walk home."

"But Dad," we chorused, "what about our Sunday dinner at the Moore's?"

"You know it's much too late for that. We will just start walking to the Oller farm, near the schoolhouse, and maybe Junior Oller will drive us home in his truck."

We took off across the hills and down the hollows, Dad carrying little Emily on his shoulders. We walked and walked for miles it seemed, and suddenly Dad brought us out into a familiar field.

"Hey, look at that, it's Aunt Mary's field!" It was the field just below our own house. Dad had tricked us into walking all the way home. Walking up one hill and down another, we kids had <u>no</u> idea where we were. I remember feeling proud that my Dad had managed that Herculean feat.

In adulthood, Emily and I are best friends. Our age difference of eight years matters not a whit in our relationship; we are close and love one another so much. We say to one another, "When we are old and probably widowed, we will live at the beach in an old shack, wear long baggy dresses and big sun hats, go barefoot, and track sand into the house." Of course that will never happen, but it's fun to pretend anyway. In 2006 Emily and Ron moved to Hilo, Hawaii and that separation has been painful. Sure, we can talk by phone anytime and e-mail at will, but it doesn't take the place of meeting her every week or so for lunch. In the meantime, when they come to the mainland, we spend every minute we can together.

My Beautiful Sister Emily

C * H * A * P * T * E * R

* 5 *

Big Barren Baptist Church

Our country church-house was up the road about a mile from our house. It was a white, clapboard building of one room with windows on three sides and two entrance doors on the fourth, facing the dirt road. In my childhood, we sat on pine benches and there was a wheezy old pump organ to accompany singing.

When Wilton was seven and I was four, my mother realized we needed some formalized Christian training and organized a Sunday School. She ordered the proper literature from the Southern Baptist Convention and persuaded Preacher Alphus Capps to come out from Doniphan. Church services were held once a month with Brother Capps providing the hellfire and damnation sermons, but we had Sunday school every week for all ages.

The church-house had previously remained quiet and vacant since the time a sect came through, called Holy-Rollers, who held meetings on some Saturday nights. They would get fired up by the Holy Ghost and sing and shout loud enough to be heard a mile away at our house. They became so high-spirited they broke out some of the windowpanes and jumped out the windows, then marched back through the doors singing, only to repeat the process. Mom was at a loss to understand how this type of worship service glorified the Lord. Dad, along with his brothers, would crack jokes about the Holy-Rollers and especially one man who, when he came into our basement grocery store and was asked what he wanted, said, "I want to get the Holy Ghost, that's what I want."

As Mother made her plans, I was terribly exhilarated to think that I was actually going to get to go to school—although just once a week. Are there isolated moments from your early life that you remember with special brilliance? I have one that is etched into my memory.

It was one summer afternoon, with white clouds floating across the brilliantly blue sky as I sat astride the fence in front of Grandma and Granddad Lewis' house, gazing across the field. The day was so clear that everything—the horizon, the far curve of the wooded hills—was edged in blue.

Pure, bottomless, meaningless joy gripped me so hard that my head swam with it. *Here I am, four years old,* I thought, *and I am going to get to go to school!* The marvelous mystique of being able to go to school and learn was something that I dreamed about and wished for.

Mom got into a little hot water with her father over a poster she placed at the front of the church, which read in bold letters, "*Whosoever Will May Come,*" I Tim. 2:4. Granddad was a strict Calvinist, although he would not have known his belief by that name. He believed that God the Father had chosen who would and who would not come to Him and that was that! Thereafter ensued a classic Biblical debate that still rages today. These are two great concepts of the Bible that seem to conflict, predestination and free will.

One incident stands out in my mind about attending Sunday worship. My mother, brother and I had walked to the church house one summer morning for services. During the morning I began to feel sick, with headache, general weakness and achiness. Not realizing how ill I was, I presume, Mom did not ask for a ride with anyone, but started us walking back home. I was so sick I could hardly put one foot in front of the other. Fever had ramped up and I ached to beat the band and found it hard to stay erect.

I managed to get to Granddad and grandma's house, about three-fourths of a mile, before Mom let me stop and lie down on the day bed in their dining room. I fell asleep and had the most horrible hallucinations; something about trying to walk on blood-red ridges to escape some inexplicable horror. It turned out that I had a virulent case of malaria which resulted in a raging fever, delirium, and the eventual inability to stand.

Every year, when warm weather arrived and mosquitoes reappeared, so did malaria. To my recollection, we did not know how to use aspirin to reduce fever. Additionally, in the remote countryside, one did not visit the doctor unless one was literally deathly sick. This time, Dad and Mom decided that I should go to Doniphan for help. A liberal administration of quinine was the remedy.

Church and Sunday services were heavily attended by the women and children of the community. Sorry to say, many of the men drove their wives to church and then stood around outside, smoking pipes and cigarettes and telling hunting and fishing stories. There were exceptions, of course, and I especially remember the brothers George and John Pigg. As I recall, it was John Pigg who stood up front to lead the singing, accompanied on the pump organ by another neighbor, Mrs. Marsh. George Pigg, the quieter brother, was in worship along with his whole family. I might add that Dad remained mostly aloof from matters sacred, not critical of them but rarely joining in worship. My own assessment of his position is that in that day and age, to some extent, religion was relegated to women, and men considered they could control their own destinies. In my father's later years I shared my opinion with him and he didn't disagree. Dad came to a formal confession of his faith as an old man and was baptized a few years before his death at eighty-six.

Both church and school were the social focal points of the community. At church we occasionally had "dinner on the ground" after Sunday services. A long picnic table was set up in the churchyard under the trees, using sawhorses with boards across the top to serve as tables. It was always a feast, with fried chicken, fried squirrel, smoked ham, potato salad, baked beans, coleslaw, sliced tomatoes, green beans, various cakes, pies and cookies. We children all knew which cook's offerings to avoid and which ones to enjoy. And needless to say, the truant men also dug right into the victuals. My favorite dish was ham, beans and cornbread:

<u>Ham and Great Northern Beans</u>
One meaty chunk of ham, bone in
One pound of dried Great Northern white beans

Cover beans with cold water and soak until soft.
Add ham to the pot with enough water to cover.
Cook gently until the beans are soft.
Ladle into individual bowls and enjoy with Missouri cornbread

<u>Missouri Cornbread</u>
1 Cup flour
1 Cup yellow cornmeal
1 tablespoon baking powder
1 teaspoon salt
1 egg
¼ cup salad oil
1-1/3 cups milk
Pour into 9 x 12 flat baking pan
Bake in 400° oven about twenty minutes until golden brown

This is my favorite meal to this day.

~ ~ ~ ~

When I was eleven years old we had a summer revival at the church and Wilton and I went forward at the invitation to indicate our acceptance of the Lord as our Savior. This was a profound experience for me and one which was preceded by much emotional conviction of my sinful nature, possibly precipitated by the hell-fire and damnation sermons. We were subsequently baptized in the Current River on the following Sunday afternoon. On that day, I waded out into the rapid current until it was about waist deep for me. And there I was properly immersed in the name of The Father, The Son and The Holy Spirit. Family and friends on the bank sang a hymn:

> Shall we gather at the river?
> Where bright angel feet have trod
> With the crystal tide forever
> Flowing by the throne of God.

> Yes we'll gather at the river,
> The beautiful, beautiful river
> Gather with the saints at the river
> That flows by the throne of God.

C * H * A * P * T * E * R

* 6 *

Big Barren School

I didn't go to kindergarten – it was not provided in Ripley County in those days. Big Barren School was located about one and one-fourth miles from home in the opposite direction from the church. Wilton and I walked, rain or shine, even on one occasion when the winter weather had dropped to twenty-eight degrees below zero. Though Dad could have driven us to school that morning, one just didn't waste gasoline on such trips. Bundling us up in extra heavy coats, mufflers, caps and gloves, Mom warned, "Don't stop anywhere; keep walking or running, or you will freeze." Since there were no telephones, Mom didn't know if we made it safely to school until we returned home that afternoon, unscathed.

Walking to school often presented problems. If the creeks were running at flood stage, we would be afraid to cross them on a makeshift bridge created by a fallen tree trunk, with the roiling and dangerous-looking waters below, so we would walk "over the hill" to school. That meant walking past Aunt Mary's house and the Old Lewis Cemetery, through the field to the hills on the south, climbing up to a safe height, turning east and walking through the woods until we judged it about the right place to drop down to the school yard. This was an arduous trek and much further than walking the dirt road directly to school. And there was always the fear that we would get lost in the woods and lose our sense of direction, an easy thing to do. Every resident had stories of people who got hopelessly lost and walked in circles as hysteria set in. Mom constantly warned us about this danger, "If you get lost, walk downhill, following a hollow or possibly a stream, and you will come out at someplace that you recognize and then you can make your way home." Thankfully we never got lost in the Ozarks.

Arriving at school and opening the door of the schoolhouse, one was assailed with smells of blackboard chalk dust, oil that was used on the bare wooden floor to keep down dust, and wood smoke from the pot-bellied stove. The school was a white clapboard building of one room, with a small cupola on the roof containing a bell. A rope from the bell hung down through the ceiling in the middle of the schoolroom to be rung by teacher or student helper before school and at the conclusion of recess and the noon hour. The school was one large room with a pot-bellied stove in the back of the room near the door, fired up by an older boy who was hired to get the room warm in cold weather before students arrived. Teacher's desk stood in front of the room with blackboards behind it. Windows on each side of the room offered natural light with which to study; there was no electricity. Above the blackboards behind teacher's desk hung an American flag and a copy of the Gilbert Stuart painting of George Washington. We had a limited supply of extracurricular books to read for pleasure. All the necessary textbooks were provided by Ripley County and the State of Missouri.

Just in front of the teacher's desk was a long bench, called a recitation bench. It provided a place for teacher to hear students in each grade recite reading, writing and arithmetic. You were expected to have done your studying and recitation preparation back at your desk. This method gave students a unique opportunity to learn the art of concentration and, also, after one's lesson was prepared, to listen to the upper grades and learn what they were studying. It was just this opportunity that allowed me to skip the sixth grade—I had already learned it all and took the Missouri State examination to pass to the next grade. Parenthetically, this presented social problems in high school when I was too young to have the same freedom for social activities that my older classmates had. In all the years I attended Big Barren School, there were never more than 22 or 23 students in all eight grades. The smallest student desks were just behind the recitation bench and larger desks were behind them, toward the rear of the schoolroom.

Despite my two years of longing to go to school, when the actual day arrived I was frightened and reluctant to go. "Why?" inquired Mom, knowing full well my dreams of reading.

"I'm afraid the kids will laugh at me because I don't know how to read," I wailed.

After Mom reassured me that the purpose of going to school was to enable me to learn, I walked out with my brother in fear and trembling to begin the next chapter of my life, proudly wearing a new red dress sewed by Mom.

The teacher always boarded with someone in the community since it was too far from town to drive every day. My first grade teacher, Miss Ann Voga, resided at our house. She drove to school every morning but Wilton and I always walked. That seems strange to me now, but I suppose the reason was that we should not appear to be teacher's pets. She was given my bedroom. I don't remember where I slept that year. Miss Ann was a very strict disciplinarian. My first infraction at school, for which I was punished by having to stay in from recess, was when I lifted my head from my books to look out the window as a vehicle passed by on the road, which, I might add, was not a frequent event.

Miss Ann started me off with my pencil in my right hand and my paper straight up and down on the desk. I am decidedly left-handed and evidently strong willed enough to persevere in changing my pencil to my left hand, because in a few weeks she let me continue with being left handed, but with the paper straight up and down on the desk and no writing upside down.

We had a teacher when I was in fifth grade, Miss Dahme, who was really from the old school, who taught us to march in various formations to music composed during the Civil War period and played on an old wind-up phonograph. These marches were then performed at the pie suppers.

Special programs were held at school at Christmas and other times of the year and afterwards we would have a "pie supper." The programs were sometimes a play with student actors, performed on a makeshift stage in the front of the schoolroom, with bed sheets strung across a high wire for a curtain. Sometimes it was music, both instrumental and vocal. My brother Wilton learned to play the harmonica, which we called a French harp, and performed it with Johnny Paul Marsh accompanying him on guitar. When I was four years old, before ever being a student, I was placed on a high stool to sing my very first solo:

> In a corner on a stool
> I sat 'cause I broke the rule.
> I'm gonna show them that I'm no fool
> With rhythm in a nursery rhyme.

An auctioneer, usually Dad, would sell the picnic boxes brought by ladies of the community. The boxes had no names on them—the ladies were supposed to keep it a secret as to which box was theirs. The boxes not only contained that cook's best culinary efforts, but the box itself was often decorated with crepe paper or colorful wrappings. The money gained from the auction was used to purchase books for extracurricular reading. The buyer of the box was granted the privilege of eating the contents with the lady who brought it. Young men and women who were romantically interested in each other would try various tricks to get to eat with their sweetheart. Events at which whole picnic dinners were prepared and auctioned were still called pie suppers.

At Christmastime, as well as having a special program, the room was decorated by us children by making red and green paper chains and hanging them on a locally-cut tree, along with tin foil decorations. As I recall, the foil was obtained from chewing gum wrappers. We never had lights on the tree since the schoolroom was not electrified.

At recess time in good weather the whole school population would often play softball or string-around, another ball game, choosing up sides and trying to get an equal number of large children and smaller children on each team. We also did other things, such as wading some in the creek, climbing trees, playing "house" by making outlines of rooms with rocks and carpeting each room with moss.

When I was in the third grade, we went down to the creek bed one day at recess where a large sycamore tree was burning. I have no idea how the fire got started, perhaps by lightning. As we stood under and around this tree, a large limb fell from the tree, knocking one boy to the ground and smashing him. His name was Zane Davis and he was Wilton's age. Wilton was one of three boys out front and got his cap knocked off by the limb. I ran as fast as my legs would carry me back to the schoolroom, dropped on my knees by my desk, crying and sobbing and asking God to save Zane's life. But it was not to be; he was taken to town to the hospital, but lived only one day. That was a horrible tragedy for all of us kids and the tragic death haunted us for a long time.

Funerals were attended by all, including children, and I learned early that death was a part of life, to be endured by trusting God for protection and for nurture and care. Most of the neighbors had little money for life's emergencies and, therefore, bodies were "laid out" and buried without embalming, with the help of friends and neighbors. My parents were always called on for help during these times. My Dad built the casket for Zane and, though I don't remember if Mom helped prepare the body for burial, she probably did. During the years we lived in the Big Barren community, all burials were in our Lewis Family Cemetery, out in the middle of Aunt Mary's field. This cemetery had no caretakers except folks in the surrounding community, and it was often in very poor condition, being overgrown with weeds and brambles. I remember many a Memorial Day when we took a picnic and flowers and went to the cemetery to rake and groom.

~ ~ ~ ~

When I was in the seventh grade after World War II had begun and many younger women had joined in the war effort, Mom returned to the classroom and became my teacher for one year at Big Barren School. She really intended to continue teaching, I think, but during the summer after that first year, Mom and Dad decided to try living in the big city by moving to Van Dyke, Michigan, near Detroit, where both Dad and Mom could work in the automobile factories which had been converted into making tanks, jeeps and other military vehicles. We never returned to Missouri to live and Mom never taught school again.

C*H*A*P*T*E*R

7

In my early years in rural Missouri, my big brother Wilton was my constant childhood companion. He was older, stronger and bigger than I and matured into a man of medium build with beautiful thick brown, wavy hair and Dad's blue eyes. I was always so proud of him. There were no children living close enough with whom we could play every day. We roamed the countryside in the summer, wading or swimming in the creek, climbing the highest trees and enjoying the forbidden fun of jumping in the hayloft in the barn. Uncle Lee, who was a life-long bachelor, at that time living with Granddad and Grandma Lewis, forbade us this activity but I don't remember that he ever caught us in the act. Once in a while we participated in another bizarre sport; smoking grapevines. The cigarette-sized vines were hollow in the center and one could draw smoke through this hollow space and then puff out smoke like men and women of the world. Mom forbade this activity but Grandma Lewis would help us light up, knowing full well that our tongues would later be so sore from drawing on these fake cigarettes that we would not want to try that activity again for a good long while.

Wilton and I quarreled a lot, perfectly normal for siblings, I suppose. But he always stood up for me when any outsider was mean or unkind. I particularly remember one instance when we were walking home from school in the early fall of the year. There was a persimmon tree in the lane bordering a field and across from Willie and Pearl Lewis's house. This tree was loaded with hard, green persimmons about the size of walnuts. Another boy who had been walking with us climbed the tree and started throwing these hard persimmons at me. My brother yelled up at him, "You'd better stop that or you'll be sorry." My heart swelled with pride and I felt protected and cared for.

Our cousin Billie Duke Henderson, son of Aunt Zelma and Uncle Zack, was a fairly frequent visitor, coming out to the country from

Doniphan. Billie was a few months younger than I and the three of us literally went wild when the Hendersons came, usually for a weekend visit. We romped all over the hills and hollers and our parents didn't worry, knowing we would eventually show up at home.

As adults, Willie, as he has been known in adulthood, someone I can go to for advice in matters of finance. He had a good career with Pacific Bell Telephone after he left the Navy. He worked his way up through the company, gaining a higher education in the process. He retired in his early fifties and decided to try a business venture. He started purchasing video game machines and placing them in pizza parlors. This resulted in a thriving business called "Randel Amusements" with a territory of most of Southern California. Our son Tom worked for him and had charge of the Los Angeles and Orange County areas. Willie eventually was ready to retire again, so he turned the business over to his oldest son, Gerry. Willie is a wise man who, with his wife Verna, my beloved sister-in-law, raised a fine family.

When our families were younger and still at home, it was the height of pleasure to get together with Willie's family for visiting and enjoyment. Our children, the cousins, grew up close in friendship which continues to this day. Willie loves music as I do, and has pursued his musical interests in barbershop singing, both quartette and chorus, and old time fiddling. He has a fine collection of violins which includes an antique from Great Grandfather William Morton Glore and a fine instrument from Uncle Nace Randel.

My Brother Willie

C * H * A * P * T * E * R

* 8 *

Lewis Cave

The Lewis limestone cave, on the Lewis family property, is just across the field and up the hill from my childhood home. This one-quarter mile long cave was always a source of pride for me. No one else in the community could boast of such a natural wonder.[3] The cave has been in the possession of the Lewis family since great-grandfather John Comer Lewis II bought the farmland and surrounding property in 1876.

It was formerly known as Big Cave or Big Barren Cave. In the early years of the twentieth century, it was a favorite recreational spot for young people in the community, who lit pine torches to find their way in the dark. Sadly, the smoke from the torches discolored much of the beauty of the cave, but in the 1930's my father electrified it and built a comfortable gravel walkway back to the end of the navigable part of the cave, past two pools of clear, cold water, containing eyeless fish and transparent, eyeless crayfish.

One particular formation grew together to form what we called "standing man," a stone column about two feet thick. How many thousands of years did it take for a stalactite and stalagmite to grow together to form this stone column? Lewis Cave was opened for business with an admission price of twenty-five cents. But Dad never made his fortune that way. The poor roads and distance from town, coupled with lack of money during the Depression, were deterrents.

---

[3]   Three and one-half miles from Current River, Lewis Cave is at least twenty feet high and fifty feet wide at its mouth, and a large spring-fed stream flows from it into Big Barren Creek one-half mile east. There are several rooms in the cave and it is noted for its stalagmites and stalactites and blind fish. *http://whmnc.umsystem.edu/exhibits/ramsay_ripley.html*

But Dad was an innovative person and he later built mushroom beds about fifty yards back from the cave entrance. The even, year-round humid climate of fifty-seven degrees was ideal for growing mushrooms. He processed and canned many of them to ship to market in St. Louis. And he peddled fresh ones to folks in Doniphan. But the 1930's of the Great Depression were not times when Americans bought many mushrooms.

My older cousins had frightened me with stories of early American Indians who once lived in the cave and, indeed, when Uncle Lee plowed the ground for the spring alfalfa crop we often found arrowheads in the field around our house. In earlier years it had also been a bear's lair.

Early one morning when I was about ten, my Mother called, "Doris Jane, time to go to the cave and get water." It was the middle of summer and our well had gone dry. But we had another source of water in our family cave, water that ran cool and pure from underground limestone sources. But it wasn't much fun for a skinny kid to bring buckets of water from the cave. It entailed walking down the gravel driveway, up the hill through heavy brush, watching for snakes, and about one hundred yards into the cave itself to the spring. In the summertime, snakes often cooled themselves in the mouth of the cave so I had to watch where I stepped.

"While you are there, bring me some butter," added my Mom. I grabbed the two-gallon zinc water bucket and headed down the driveway in the humid and sunny morning that promised to turn into a hot and miserable midsummer day.

In my early years we didn't have a refrigerator, so dairy products were kept cool in the cave. It was a happy day when I was about ten when we got a refrigerator. But water and butter, hot weather and snakes turned out not to be my concerns that morning.

As I entered the darkness of the mouth of cave, the cool humidity felt pleasant on my skin. But then I heard it, a loud phantom voice, "WHOOOOOO." I didn't waste even a half-second, but turned tail and ran for dear life down the hillside and back to the house. Mom was busy preparing breakfast in the hot, steamy kitchen. "Doris Jane, where are the butter and water I sent you for?" I didn't reply, but just turned around and reluctantly, in fear and trepidation, headed back for the cave.

Taking no chances, I began to make a lot of noise as I climbed the short distance from road to cave entrance. Singing at the top of my voice, I was not about to let anything "get" me while in the cave. I entered the cave, still singing and shouting, and made my way to the furthermost point, the spring, to get the water. I then retreated to the platform that held the dairy products, then backed my way out of the cave and raced down the hill to the safety of home.

What was that strange noise? I *know* I heard it; it wasn't a figment of my imagination. I never told my parents. A practical answer would be that a cow, standing in the stream that exited the cave about one hundred yards below the entrance of the cave, made itself heard and the sound carried up through the watercourse, perhaps getting distorted on the way into the cave itself.

Our house had electricity provided by a generator Dad had placed in the cave, stringing electrical wires from cave to the house. His expertise in building this electrical system came from the time he tended batteries in the Chevrolet plant in St. Louis, plus a set of electrical engineering books.

So we had "luxuries" such as a wringer washing machine in the basement and a big deluxe model Sears and Roebuck radio. Mind you, we did not have indoor plumbing, so Mom had to carry water by the bucketful from our back yard pump to fill the washing machine in the basement.

Nevertheless, in my formative years, I had the distinct impression that we were rich. Since wealth is a relative thing, I guess we were, as we certainly had more of the comforts of life than folks in our neighboring community. Neighbors often came over to our house on Saturday night to listen to the Grand Old Opry on our radio.

C * H * A * P * T * E * R

* 9 *

HOME LIFE – DAD'S COUNTRY STORE

Sitting at the kitchen table with Mom at the old iron cook stove, we listened as she cooked, regularly lecturing us on how we would assume leadership in the community when we became adults. The Bible teaches that to whom much has been given, much will be required,[4] and it was expected that, in time, we would step up to the plate and become community leaders. Like Mom's parents before her, the whole neighborhood looked up to our family and turned to Mom and Dad for advice and help in time of need. Elmer served on the school board and more than once had neighbors paroled to him who had gotten in trouble with the law. Dad once had Old Man Grubbs paroled to him after he had gotten in trouble with the law. The Grubbs family included about ten children who never had quite enough to eat and Dad helped them out more than once with staple food items from our little basement grocery store "on credit." Once when Dad had taken him to town, Old Man Grubbs came back with a whole ham, a rare treat for the Grubbs family. Later, he told Dad this story:

"I got home about midnight with that ham and it looked so good I decided to slice off a little tidbit, fry and eat it before I went to bed. One by one those children smelled that wonderful aroma and got up to share in the treat. We ate on that ham all night and boiled the bone for breakfast."

Dad offered rides to Doniphan for twenty-five cents each. Often, those who rode along with Dad would come back with groceries, and sometimes would purchase soda pop and other unnecessary foodstuffs. This would hurt my Dad's feelings, since they oftentimes owed him money from purchases in our basement store. Dad never turned away

---

[4]   Romans 6:32

a needy person, but would help out in some way to keep the families fed. It might be dry beans, flour or cornmeal. If the neighbor came to our basement store and brought something to trade, such as a few eggs, he would take what they had and give them goods in exchange. Dad tested the eggs himself and if they were not fresh, would simply discard them. Fresh eggs were taken to Doniphan to sell.

Dad never applied for government assistance, as many in the county did, but managed to make a living through various entrepreneurial projects, such as selling groceries, selling gas and oil, raising chickens using the latest methods, waking them at 3:00 A. M. with a homemade alarm clock device that automatically turned the lights on in the chicken house so they would begin eating. He sent off to the Department of Agriculture for the latest methods of raising chickens for their eggs. He followed the suggestion of experts, feeding the chickens the right mix of chicken mash and ground oyster shells to harden the egg shells. He constructed home-made automatic feeders and a watering device from materials on hand.

He began raising mushrooms in our cave, and electrifying the cave to make it a tourist attraction. Perhaps, though, he replenished the family larder best by using his stake-bed truck to haul railroad ties to Doniphan for men in the community, who cut the timber off their land and hacked them out with an axe.

Summers were probably the best time of year, despite the heat and pests such as mosquitoes, gnats, ticks, chiggers and, the fearsome poisonous snakes. I loved summertime because my cousins would come from the city on their summer holiday and we would have playmates every day. I have literally dozens of first cousins, some of whom I never knew, who were old enough to be my parents. But other younger cousins came every summer and we became friends and sometimes pen pals. Probably the cousins from St. Louis came most often. My Mom would work her head off cooking for the visiting families, especially Uncle Chester and Aunt Opal Lewis cousins, Marilyn, Al, Gene, Bob, Dot and Frank. Imagining that they needed extra nourishment, she filled them up with fresh garden produce, cornbread, lots of biscuits and home-made jelly and jam, fried chicken, fresh fish, squirrel and rabbit. Dad would take us on excursions to Current River for swimming and boating in his home-made jon boat and great picnic feasts. We all ran amok in the woods and fields, the kids from the city especially enjoying the freedom of wide open spaces.

~ ~ ~ ~

As an enterprise to keep financially afloat during The Great Depression without government assistance, Dad opened a small country store in the basement of our house. As I recall, it only had the basic staples needed in any country household, such as flour, cornmeal, sugar, coffee, tea, tobacco in the can, and some cigarettes. But the country men mostly rolled their own cigarettes for economy's sake. He also had a keg or two of the most common sizes of nails and sold gasoline and oil. He would measure each gallon of gasoline in a measuring can with a spout and pour it into the customer's gas tank. Dad kept a set of books and in many instances gave people food "on credit" and was never paid. Dad was a real country philanthropist in this regard and when he closed the store, the books were closed forever. I don't believe he ever made much money from this endeavor, but it provided a place for the neighbors to get food and fuel without having to go to town.

The biggest temptation in the store to Wilton and me was the small stock of candy and gum. We were each granted five cents a week allowance, and, of course, about the only place to spend our allowance was in Dad's store. On Saturday mornings, allowance day, we would first have breakfast and then hot-foot it down to the basement to choose our candy. That bowl of oatmeal looked so much bigger on Saturday morning. But we were required to finish it before getting our treat. At Christmastime Dad would stock more candies, including hard Christmas candy and "chocolate drops" in large glass apothecary jars. There were a few occasions when we couldn't stand the temptation and would snitch some candy and hide out behind the house to eat it. Of course we never got away with it.

Dad caught us one fine day. "Wilton and Doris Jane, since you have been eating candy out behind the house that you stole from the store, you will have to be punished. Go out and cut your own switches and bring them to me."

I wasn't very old at the time and could not, for the life of me, find a switch. Spying some boards in the wood yard, I dragged one of them into the house for the requisite punishment. But I didn't escape the inevitable, because hardly concealing a grin, Dad administered the proper punishment with my brother's switch.

Normally, Dad was the parent of choice to administer corporal punishment, but I especially remember one occasion when Mom, totally exasperated with the two of us, switched us with dead onion stalks after Wilton and I got into a fight in the garden while pulling onions for fall storage. To this day I remember the prolonged stinging in my lower legs from that event.

The folks in the community who came to the store were, by and large, simple country farmers, but there was a sprinkling of some colorful people. I remember Saree Davis, an old lady who chewed tobacco. She carried two purses, one for her money and the other to be used as a portable spittoon. Mom always appreciated her, because Old Lem Lewis (no relation) would spit his tobacco juice into a corner of the basement store. Later Mom would say, "I just wish he would spit in the middle of the floor, it would be easier to clean up." Lem was an old curmudgeon whose farmhouse was near our school. One day he arrived at our store about dinnertime and Mom invited him to stay and eat. Thereafter we noticed a possible trend; Lem started to make a habit of arriving about mealtime. Mom had to be creative to discourage his regular appearance at our table.

One day Nellie Bridge came walking over the field with a basket of eggs for trade in the store. She had wonderful news. "Edna Mae, my daughter Bonnie got married the other day. She didn't git much of a man but she shore got some nice furniture."

One evening rather late, Luther and Charlie Brooks came rushing into the basement store, eyes bulging and faces beet red. "What can I do for you fellows?" inquired Dad. Both talking at once, they exclaimed, "Elmer, we just saw a headless woman run across the road in front of our truck. Luther was driving and almost ran over her. She floated right up the bank on the other side of the road. It was a ghost!"

"Now boys, you know there isn't any such thing."

"Well, we saw her. You just come with us and we'll look for her up there."

Taking note of their agitated demeanor and obvious fright, Dad replied, "OK, if you insist, I'll go with you."

Away they went up the road towards the church house. As their truck lights hit a mud hole in the middle of the road, a reflection of the lights flew up the bank. No headless women – just a mirror image of headlights floating up the clay bank.

From time to time a traveling sawmill crew, employees of a large lumber company, came to the community, settling for a brief time in a wooded area that could be cut and milled. The crew often had families with them and they lived in tents and the children attended Big Barren School. One day two of these little girls came to Dad's store with a small amount of money to purchase flour or sugar. Mom felt sorry for them and offered some vegetables from her garden, telling the girls to pick some tomatoes and green beans. They happily took a paper sack and went into the garden. Much later, one called to the other, "Irene, did you pick everything?"

A large family named Buffington owned a farm over on Current River. The parents had a novel way of naming the children in their ever-expanding family. Using the alphabet, they started naming their children with AB, then CD and so on. So the oldest children's names were Ada Bell and Cora Dell. By the time I arrived as a citizen of Ripley County, the current owner of the farm was a son—way down the line of the alphabet. His name was Ura Vincent.

Flour and cornmeal were sold in colorful cloth sacks of twenty-five or fifty pounds, printed with small, pastel flowers. The ladies of the community would purchase enough flour or cornmeal to enable them to make a new dress from the sacks. Many a lady walked the country roads and trails in these home-sewn creations and they often saw similar prints on other women and girls at church on Sunday.

~ ~ ~ ~

GOING HUNTING

"Wilton, take this pan and go up to the attic and fill it with peanuts. I want to put them into the oven while the stove is still hot from cooking supper." Dad didn't need to ask twice. As he took off for the attic, Wilton anticipated an evening with good warm nuts on which to snack. Our big country kitchen was warm and cozy on this cold night. Even though the windows were bare and the rest of the house without heat, the heat emanating from the old iron cook stove was enough to keep us cozy and comfortable.

"I'm going 'coon hunting tonight with Bud," Dad mentioned, as he went to the closet for his heavy hunting coat and gun. It would take at least an hour for the peanuts to roast, so there was no hurry, but Dad loved this one sport that he allowed himself after a day of hard work making a living in the Great Depression of the 1930's.

Waiting for the peanuts to roast, Dad settled into his chair in the warm kitchen while my brother and I sat at the kitchen table doing our homework. Mom sat nearby, knitting needles clacking in the dim light from the one overhead, bare light bulb. A delicious nutty aroma filled the room as we turned on the radio to listen to one of our favorite programs, *Lux Radio Theater*, an hour-long drama. Dad got up to stir the peanuts every few minutes to assure they roasted evenly. He may have been a strong outdoors man, but when the radio drama descended into a sad episode, Dad was the first to grab his red bandana handkerchief out of his back pocket to wipe a tear from his eyes. As Dad settled back, I noticed his coarse, thick, wavy hair that he combed straight off his wide forehead, revealing a slightly receding hairline and big ears.

Dad and his friends and relatives all had marvelous coon hunting stories and when men got together, it was almost always one of the main topics of conversation. Dad would fill his pockets with roasted peanuts, take Old Spot and his gun and strike off through the winter woods, dark, cold and dripping wet sometimes, to hunt coon. He would stay out for hours at a time, coming home in the wee hours of the morning and then getting up to milk cows at the usual early hour.

As *Lux Radio Theater* signed off, Dad took his peanuts out of the oven and filled his pockets with the warm nuts. He picked up his gun and walked out into the dark night to whistle to Spot that they were going hunting. I might mention that in the country where there are <u>no</u> city lights, nighttime is black as midnight velvet. Some of the coon hunting stories included those of hunters who lost their way in the woods and had to wait for daybreak to find their way out. Spot was an old 'coon-hunting hound who resisted chasing rabbits or deer but headed for the woods to search for 'coon. He bayed as he went, signaling to Dad the direction he was going. Soon Spot changed his bark to a long, keening howl, "Yow- yow, yooooooooooo," his signal that he had a 'coon treed. Dad and our neighbor Bud Lewis were in business. Conversely, if your dog got distracted and started chasing deer or rabbits, he was literally in the dog house and was often traded off for another. After a successful night catching one or more coons, the pelts were stretched and dried and then sold for their fur. I really don't think Dad ever cared about what little money he made on pelts; the name of the game was the fun of the hunt.

I never went on one of these dark-night forays—it was strictly for men—but I heard stories for years at country social gatherings and family reunions. The women talked quilting, gardening and babies, and the men told 'coon hunting stories. It seems that the raccoon is a sporty, fighting, creature, who never gives up without a good scrap. When Wilton was eleven or twelve years old, Dad taught him to use the 22 rifle. The day came when he was allowed to go hunting alone and take Old Spot. As much as he loved to hunt, however, Spot wouldn't go. We were sure he felt that Wilton was <u>not</u> old enough to carry the 22 and shoot it. But in recent years, my brother confessed that he had previously shot at Spot with his be-be gun. No wonder Old Spot wouldn't go hunting with him.

C * H * A * P * T * E * R

* 10 *

Doris Jane, About Four

EVERYDAY LIFE IN THE OZARKS

When I was growing up in the 1930's, it was generally believed fresh air was beneficial to good health. Mom and Dad therefore often had us sleep on the screened-in back porch, even in wintertime. Sometimes in winter I would awaken to find snow drifted through the screen and onto the blankets and quilts. After Dad arose in the morning and started the fire in the kitchen stove, he then called us to get up and you can believe we made a speedy run for the kitchen door through the smattering of snow. It was just a few steps.

We also slept on feather beds, which were big, puffy comforters and into which we sank after climbing into bed. Imagine the allergies! It was known as "The Ague" back then, and we didn't realize it was caused by the feathers. When I was eight or nine, Dad built a home-made furnace for the house. He put a large fifty gallon oil drum in the basement, made a giant sized flue with sheet metal which reached up to the floor above, then cut a hole in the living room floor and put a metal grate over it. I thought it was quite a luxury. Previously, we stayed in the kitchen and when bedtime came, we made a quick exit to our beds and got under those covers as soon as possible. Of course, it couldn't have been that cold, because the brick chimney to which the kitchen stove flue was connected went up through the upper floor and out the roof, so radiant heat from the chimney must have partially heated the upstairs bedrooms.

Winter also brought another treat—home made ice cream. Even though the cows did not produce milk in winter, Mom made ice cream mix from canned evaporated milk. We had lots of ice handy from icicles hanging off the roof. These were crushed and put in the big old zinc wash tub, which, incidentally, was also our bathtub. The ice cream mixture was poured into a one gallon syrup bucket with tight-fitting lid. This nested in the ice and rock salt in the zinc wash tub and then turned back and forth by the handle until we had ice cream. Wonderfully delicious!

Christmastime meant we could go out in the woods and choose our own Christmas tree. Sometimes it seemed we walked for miles to select the perfect one. We may have had one or two strands of lights for our tree, but mostly we made our own decorations after the style of those made at school. Mom made special treats such as home-made candy and we always had fresh oranges from town. We had plenty of black walnuts for baking because we picked them up ourselves, cracked the extremely hard shell and picked out the kernels with a small nail. Occasionally I had a walnut and butter sandwich for school lunch, which I thought was special, but I believe Mom felt it was a last resort for a sandwich filling, so we didn't get it very often.   As I recall, we usually had a sled, but I never learned to ice skate with anything but the bottoms of my shoes or boots.

Springtime brought rain, rain, rain and with the snow melt we had floods most every year. This meant the creek runs were full to overflowing, the Current River was up, and some years we had overflowing creeks, coming right down through the field in front of our house and often getting into the basement. It presented problems in getting the truck out of the country and to town (nothing but dirt [mud] roads and no bridges over the creeks; they had to be forded). Walking to school also presented a problem. If the creeks were high, we would be afraid to cross them on a makeshift bridge created by a fallen tree trunk, so we would go "up over the hill" to school. This meant a much longer walk over past Aunt Mary's house, past the Lewis cemetery, and up the hill behind Aunt Mary's fields; walking from one hill to another on a ridge and being careful not to get too far back in the hills.

It was a very easy thing to get lost in the Ozarks, and every resident had stories of people who had gotten hopelessly lost and went temporarily berserk. We were taught that if we got lost in the woods to always go downhill, and if possible, follow a stream. Theoretically one would come out at a road or a river. I never got lost in the woods.

Springtime also found us in the thicket behind the garden, looking for the first wild onions, violets and buttercups and wading in the remnants of the creek that meandered through the thicket. Gathering wild greens was always happily anticipated because we would be really hungry for fresh green things after subsiding all winter on canned food. Mom would take me out into the fields to teach me which wild greens were edible such as lamb's quarter, dock, polk and dandelion.

I recently saw a course for college credit being offered which taught one to recognize and harvest wild greens. I'll bet I could teach that course! Dad gathered wild mushrooms. Since there were also many poisonous varieties, he would never allow us to pick mushrooms, but did that himself. They had an absolutely marvelous flavor and tasted entirely different from domestically raised ones.

When the weather warmed and the creeks receded, there were always pools of water left for a couple of months (we called them "holes") where we could find fish, crawdads and had wonderful opportunities to swim. Unfortunately, Mom was deathly afraid of water and so our swimming times were limited. However, on more than one occasion, we took a swim without her knowledge, stripping down to bare skin so wet clothes wouldn't betray us. I believe her fear of the water came from the dangers of Current River whose name aptly describes the condition of that river. As a child I never swam in Current River, but because our mother's fear of the river was transferred to us, we were in fear and trembling as we watched the adults swimming in the river.

~ ~ ~ ~

When summer arrived, one of Dad's favorite leisure activities was to go boating on the river. He had a home-made jon boat, which was a dory-type boat, pointed in front and squared off in the back with slats for seats in the middle part of the boat. He had an outboard motor on the back of the boat to take us on delightful rides on the river. The river was not only swift but was a veritable hodgepodge of snags, fallen tree trunks and changing currents. The river changed course constantly and one had to know where the deep channels were to get around the hazards.

Elmer in Heaven

Visiting relatives from the city in summer meant that we could go to the river and usually take a picnic supper. These wonderful picnics appeared as if by magic, but now that I'm an adult I can imagine all the hot times Mom spent in the kitchen, preparing this delectable food. There were simple picnic facilities at Gooseneck, a park on the river, about three miles from home. There was a boat launch and also picnic tables under a roof. On occasion, Mom hired Jessie Burroughs, a local girl, to help with these gargantuan feasts.

Dad also loved to go gigging at night on the river. He and his fishing buddies would light a torch and place it in the front of the boat and when fish came up to investigate the light, they were gigged by the sportsmen, using a spear with a rope on the end of the handle to prevent losing the gig in the river. In the same manner, they would also gig huge bullfrogs from the riverbanks as they croaked their nighttime songs. Breakfasts of fried fish and fried frog legs, which had been coated in cornmeal, were part of standard summer breakfast fare.

This was a normal thing, but now I find my children are horrified that I would eat frog legs, and especially for breakfast! I suspect they are equally horrified that we ate squirrel during the season. Dad loved to hunt and Old Spot was equally wild about hunting. In fact, when Dad returned home after going to town for the day, Old Spot would take off up the hillside and start barking up a tree, to try and tempt Dad to go hunting with him. Spot's dash up the hillside often announced Dad's imminent arrival, even before we could hear the truck motor with our human ears. Dad never killed more squirrels than we could eat and if he happened to come home with several, Mom would can them in quart glass jars and we would have squirrel in the wintertime.

What other mischievous things did we do in the summertime? Well, for one thing, we dearly delighted in jumping off the rafters of the barn down into the freshly gathered hay. Uncle Lee strictly forbade us to do that, but one of us would keep watch while the other one jumped and perhaps we loved it because it was such a forbidden delight. The hay was sticky and oftentimes dusty and I'm sure burying ourselves in that hay didn't help our allergies any. We were never forbidden to climb trees, and we would climb way up in some of them—especially sycamores. My recollection is that we could get 20 or 30 feet up. We never fell.

We had a swing out in back of the garden in an old wild cherry tree, which held us for many a great time of swinging. I always think of this cherry tree and swing when I read a poem by Robert Louis Stevenson from his *A Child's Garden of Verses:*

> How do you like to go up in a swing,
> Up in the air so blue?
> Oh, I do think it the pleasantest thing
> Ever a child can do!

I became an avid reader at an early age. Every time Mom went to town she would bring me an armload of books from the Doniphan Public Library. I often got books I had already read, and I sometimes wondered if I had read every child's book in the library. This love of reading has carried through my whole life and to this day I usually have my nose in a book at any leisure moment.

I hope Mom enjoyed gardening, because she planted a huge garden every spring. She carefully tended it and then spent many a hot summer's day in the kitchen, canning her produce. We always had canned corn, tomatoes, green beans, peas, spinach, potatoes and sometimes more exotic vegetables like okra. There were onions, radishes and strawberries too. She also canned something she called soup mix which was a mixture of all of the above vegetables, and this made a great winter dinner. Her shelves in the basement were always full of delectable things to eat, stored for the winter months. We also went berry picking around the time of my birthday, July 8, and canned all the blackberries we could find. Mom and Dad also bought peaches at a peach orchard near town to can for winter fruit for about a dollar a bushel. Also, there was an old peach orchard, planted in the woods on the side of the Aunt Mary Hill, set out by an earlier Lewis, possibly my great-grandfather John Comer II. We visited that old peach orchard and picked peaches until time and neglect caused the trees to die.

When fall arrived, it was time to butcher hogs for use in the winter. I always hated this day, because Dad had to shoot the hogs with his gun, then gut, scald and scrape the hair off the skin. I really didn't mind any of it except the shooting. Mom and Grandma would build a fire under the old black iron wash kettle in Grandma's yard and they would dunk the hairy skin in the boiling water and the hair would usually come right off. Nothing was wasted; the fatty skin was cut into chunks and baked in the oven to render out the fat which was used to make soap. The hams and bacon were smoke cured in Grandma and Granddad's smoke house, where they hung all winter to be used when needed. The remainder of the meat was canned in quart glass jars. This pork was our staple, which was augmented by squirrel, rabbit, fish, chickens and, in season, wild venison. I never learned to like beef until our "city" years; I think it was because we never ate it in the country.

Halloween in the Missouri Ozarks never was for costumes and trick or treat forays. It was strictly for trying to scare people. One year Mom said, "Let's go out on Halloween night and scare some folks." Wilton fashioned a tin can with a hole in one end large enough to string some strong twine through it. He then coated the string with resin and when drawing his finger and thumb along the string, could make a screechy sound. We set out in the dark night for the first house. Try to imagine nothing but moon and stars to light your way—no artificial light of any kind in the country and the stars were almost shocking in their brightness without city lights to dilute the effect. Some stars were like huge, burning silver flowers hanging so close you could almost touch them; then there was the silver peppering of smaller stars, the diamond-dusted arc of the Milky Way, Big and Little Dippers and the stars by which seamen navigated for centuries.

We arrived at our first house after a walk of about twenty minutes. Hiding behind trees in the yard, Wilton drew his finger and thumb along his home-made screecher and produced a loud, eery sound. In the house we heard a hushed voice, "What was that?" Glenn Davis came to the door and looked out. We all yelled, "Happy Halloween! Now we're walking over to Fletch and Mary's house to scare them." Glenn turned around and called Noma, his wife, "Let's go too." So they pulled the sheets off their beds to wrap themselves like ghosts, and we all started through a section of heavy woods towards Fletch and Mary's. About half way there we heard voices. It was a couple of the Davis boys, walking down the road in the inky night to scare someone else. "Quick, hide in the trees, and let's scare them," Glenn whispered.

"Reeeeeeeeekkkkkk" went Wilton's tin can.

Glenn stepped out and flapped his arms under the sheet.

"Eldon, there's a ghost out there in those trees, see it?" cried Dorse. "Let's get out of here."

They turned and ran as fast as they could for home.

Next day at school Eldon and Dorse were full of their ghost story. We never said a word.

~ ~ ~ ~

JENNY THE DONKEY AND OTHER PETS

When Dad started a commercial mushroom operation, he built large raised beds about fifty feet back in the cave, putting in the proper mix of loamy soil and fertilizers, and planting the spores. He needed help in getting all the soils into the cave, so he bought a little donkey we promptly named Jenny. At first attempt Jenny refused to go into the cave. She was probably unfamiliar with the damp, earthy smell and may have been afraid of the dark corners beyond the reach of the electric lights. Dad had to use some ingenuity with Jenny. He blindfolded her, put a bucket of her favorite grain under her nose and, when she took a step forward to get the treat, backed up with the bucket of grain until he had her completely into the cave. He then removed the blindfold and allowed her to eat her treat. After that, she seemed unafraid and willingly carried whatever Dad needed into the cave.

Dad's mushroom venture wasn't very successful. Most residents of Doniphan were simple folks who didn't cook with mushrooms. Even though he sold some to the local aristocracy, and though he canned, labeled and tried to peddle canned mushrooms on the St. Louis market, he never had any real success at it. For awhile we ate lots of mushrooms.

Jenny, provided a good source of fun and recreation for Wilton and me. We climbed on and rode her, used her as a beast of burden to carry sacks of walnuts, and generally treated her as a pet. She regularly bucked Wilton off her back. But because of my size she never offered to buck me off. I prided myself by saying, "She knows I'm a girl." One hot day in late summer we went up the road to gather black walnuts for winter storage. When we had loaded our sack with the largest ones and, grunting and straining, lifted the sack onto her back, Jenny bucked the sack off. She repeated this maneuver several times until we stomped home in a rage. "Mom," we complained together, "Old Jenny won't carry the walnuts but just bucks them off her back." Mom came up through the field to the walnut tree, took a large stick, shook it in front of Jenny's eyes: "Jenny, do you want to get whammed with this stick?" With not another protest, Jenny meekly carried the sack of walnuts home.

Dad and Uncle Zack once had a contest to see who could ride Jenny the longest without getting bucked off. Uncle Zack was not very tall, and he got bucked off immediately. When Dad got on, he locked his feet and legs under Jenny's belly and Jenny couldn't get rid of him. Dad won the cigar.

We had some other interesting and perhaps some surprising pets in the country. The principal pet was, of course, our hound dog, Old Spot, but we also had a pet crow that Dad had brought home as a baby bird and which we raised to adulthood. We named him Mike and taught him to say "hello." He was an inveterate thief, and would pick up any shiny object and make away with it.

Mom found Mike's treasure trove of shiny nails, thimbles, and other shiny objects under a gunny sack in the garden which she had put down to keep the strawberry plants from freezing. He used to follow us to school, cawing loudly and flying high through the trees, with the intent of eating the wild bird seed we school children had put out. We could never get him to go home, even though we yelled and threw rocks at him. He met his maker one night in a tall tree behind our wood yard, probably at the hand and paws of a 'possum.

I also once had a pet pig, the runt of a litter. When this tiny pig, never named, almost drowned one night in a rainstorm and Dad brought him into the basement, placed him in a box and gave him a shot of medicinal whiskey. The piglet got drunk and unable to stand started squealing, falling around in the box much to the delight of Wilton and me. I raised him on household slops until he was bigger than I was. My Dad bought him from me for six dollars to replace a pig he had accidentally run over and killed one day on the road to town. I felt cheated, only six dollars after months of work, carrying those heavy buckets of slops to feed him.

We enjoyed other casual pets that paraded through our lives. We had two turkeys once; they were so dumb they wouldn't come in out of the rain and had to be caught and carried to safety. Dad once brought home a baby raccoon. We caged him under the front porch, which was enclosed with latticework. He was so wild he wouldn't eat or drink. When we attempted to give him water in a pottery soup bowl he bit a plug out of it. The bowl was thereafter known as the coon bowl.

When we were in Doniphan in 1993, Aunt Rose Randel gave me a little bowl that was the same pattern as the "coon bowl," that I keep for memories. Needless to say we didn't keep the coon. We once cut our initials on the shell of a wild terrapin and years later he walked out of the woods and back into our lives.

Wild animals in the Missouri Ozarks included panther, greatly feared. Most every old timer had a story of a panther or bobcat stalking him. They have an unearthly scream which would put fear into any human being. Deer, rabbits, squirrels, raccoon, fox and, of course, our most feared, snakes, abounded. We were taught at a very early age the dangers of stepping anywhere before we looked, for fear that we would step on a snake. They hibernated in cold weather months, but when the weather warmed up, watch out. There were numerous non-poisonous ones, but the most feared were rattlesnakes and copperheads. And on the river we could see poisonous cottonmouths swimming in the water or sunning themselves on a fallen log. Wilton and I always killed every snake we came across, believing that it was our duty to decrease the snake population wherever and whenever possible. We only succumbed to terror once when in the woods playing; saw a large snake coiled in front of our path and ran home like the wind, convinced it was chasing us. It wasn't.

The method of snake assassination had to be swift and deadly or he would retaliate by striking out at us. First, stun the snake with a large stick or rock, followed rapidly by mashing its head off. We always looked around for handy weapons before initiating the kill. These days it is not environmentally correct to kill snakes, but we didn't know that then.

It would be easy to forget about the pesky ticks and chiggers abounding in summer. But they were a reality and we contended with them daily. I think I hated the seed ticks most, they would invade my legs, marching up over feet and ankles by the hundreds. We would find pennyroyal, an aromatic weed, to switch these critters off us.

Perhaps this is the time to be candid, and tell you the old timers in the community always killed deer for venison, both in and out of season. I never liked to eat it, but we had venison rather regularly. It was called goat meat by one and all, supposedly to protect us from the game warden. And, to the credit of those country folk, only enough deer were killed to provide meat on the table; they were never killed just for sport.

On one memorable occasion, when Uncle Zack, Aunt Zelma and our cousin Billy Duke came out to the country from town for the weekend, the men went hunting early on Sunday morning. Later, the preacher was invited to Grandma's house for Sunday dinner after church. Unbeknownst to us kids, the men had killed a "goat" and laid the carcass out on a pile of lumber up behind Grandma's house about fifty yards back in the woods. We kids, running wild in these woods and playing with wild abandon as usual when Billy came, found this carcass and ran down to the house, loudly proclaiming, "Grandma, we found a deer carcass on the lumber pile up by the henhouse." One of the women, working in the kitchen with Grandma, and being embarrassed at our discovery and the consequent infraction of the law, shushed us up, "You didn't see anything like that, kids." With loud voices, easily heard in the living room where the preacher sat waiting for a call to dinner, we shouted, "We did too, just come with us and we'll show you." Nothing would quiet us. We kids stuck to our story, much to the embarrassment of our parents and probably the amusement of the preacher. Grandma took us outside in the back yard. "You kids need to keep quiet because the preacher is in the living room with the rest of the family."

And, speaking of calling it goat meat, Uncle Zack and Dad once did a real number on Uncle Zack's brother, Waif. Waif owned a goat that kept eating the food in the livestock sale barn in Doniphan, run by Uncle Zack to buy and sell livestock. Zack kept warning Waif, "You've got to keep that goat away from the feed, he's eating up the profits." One day, when once more the goat got into the feed, Uncle Zack loaded the goat into the back of his pickup and brought it out to the country, where he and Dad butchered the goat and Mom canned it in glass jars. Uncle Zack took Waif some of the canned meat, "Here, Waif, have some freshly canned goat meat." Naturally, Waif thought he was getting illegal venison. Uncle Zack never told him any different nor did he ever tell him what happened to his goat.

Years later when Dick and I were visiting Ripley County, Dick went to the sale barn one morning to see how Uncle Zack auctioned off his livestock. He was sitting up in the stands and enjoying the spectacle when Uncle Zack led a young heifer into the ring. Dick, wanting to make himself known to Uncle Zack, waved happily. "Sold," shouted the auctioneer. Dick had just bought himself a nice heifer. Thankfully Uncle Zack was able to correct the situation, and you can believe that Dick didn't do any more waving that morning.

~ ~ ~ ~

I have mentioned the violets and buttercups in the woods behind our back garden. It was such a joy to find them blooming away in the cold spring earth—we were always *so* tired of the drab and grey winter scene. Besides the glorious early spring blooming of the redwood and dogwood trees, honeysuckle bloomed in the woods and we would go hunting for this wild variety of azalea which had the most marvelous perfume.

The hillside across the field from Aunt Ann's place had a stand of wild honeysuckle and we always made a pilgrimage to see and pick them. Wild onions sprang up in the fields also, and the cattle would eat them and their milk would consequently taste faintly of onion.

In the fall of the year, of course, the woods were a radiant mass of yellow, orange and red, with evergreen trees mixed in for variety in the autumn bouquet. When walking through the woods, one could always come across one more tree that seemed more colorful then the last. Nowadays people travel to New England to see the fall color, but I tell you that it simply couldn't be more lovely than autumn in the Missouri Ozarks, those venerable old mountains are considered by geologists to be some of the oldest mountains in the world.

In more recent years we took the whole family to visit Ripley County. It was the last week of October and the trees were in riotous color. A quick change in the weather resulted in a nice snowfall and we got to feast our eyes on the most unusual happening, snow piled upon the trees still displaying their fall colors.

C * H * A * P * T * E * R

* 11 *

MUSIC

Ever since I can remember I have loved music and have had a deep passion to perform music in some form or another, listening, singing or playing *something*. It is a testimony of God's love for me that I have had wonderful musical opportunities, both to learn and to perform music. As a small child I remember sitting at the kitchen table and pretending it was a piano, plunking my fingers up and down the edge of the table. "Watch me, mamma, I am playing the piano." And when we went to Naylor to visit Dad's sister and brother-in-law Aunt Ollye, Uncle Arthur and their family, I must have driven them to distraction banging on their piano.

My first musical listening experiences were extremely limited - Grand Old Opry on radio and old Baptist hymns at church and Sunday School, plus, of course, the ditties my Dad sang for our amusement. He had quite a repertoire of songs and poetry he learned in his younger years, and he never forgot a word of any of them. He taught Wilton, Emily and me these songs. Some of them were entitled: *Buffalo Gal, Arawanna, Sally Goodin*. Many of these old songs can be found on the Internet. I believe a lot of Dad's music came from Irish folk music which had been carried west to Missouri by settlers from Tennessee in the covered-wagon train that brought some of my family. Certainly the fiddle music was of Irish origin and a few of those jigs and reels had words. Dad made an attempt at playing fiddle, guitar and French harp or harmonica, but never mastered any. He was a singer.

Uncle Nace, Dad's brother, turned out to be the accomplished fiddler in the family. I am proud to say Wilton has a collection of old violins, including Uncle Nace's old fiddle. He plays them with not a small measure of accomplishment, winning many fiddle contests and even acting as judge in others. In his collection of violins, he has another instrument of significance to the family, Great Grandpa Glore's violin, a conservatory model made in Cremona, Italy circa 1850. It is a mystery to the family how William Morton Glore acquired this instrument. He was a Private in the Union Army during the War Between the States and otherwise spent his life as a simple country farmer in Washington County, Missouri and later in Ripley County.

It is likely that he learned to read music by the *Sacred Harp*, an early American musical genre surviving to this day. Itinerant music teachers used to ply their trade in the rural south by going from community to community, selling their songbooks for ten or fifteen cents and holding music schools at the local church or school. *Sacred Harp* relies on powerful rhythm and strong harmonies to belt out some of America's favorite hymns. It is a communal experience, not necessarily a performance. To this day participants gather for day-long singings with lots of food. They sit in a square and sing to God and for mutual enjoyment.[5]

Dad's older brother, Uncle Bob, was also a good singer, a tenor, and when the two of them got together, it was always a music fest. We once visited Uncle Bob and Aunt Frieda in St. Louis when immediately after supper Dad and Uncle Bob started singing. Uncle Bob had an old gospel hymnbook with songs in it that you never heard before or since—really quite unsophisticated lyrics but good harmonies. Songs such as *Will the Circle Be Unbroken, or Papa Sang Bass, Mama Sang Tenor.* The whole household went to bed to the sound of their singing and we later learned they had sung almost all night. Reluctantly they finally went to bed, but as the next day dawned, they were heard singing from their respective beds, with the long suffering wives lying alongside them probably in misery and considering murder.

---

[5] http://en.Wikipedia.org/wiki/Sacred_Harp.

C*H*A*P*T*E*R

* 12 *

Wartime and Changes

I first learned about World War II by reading the horror on my Father's face as he sat listening to the radio news of the Pearl Harbor bombing on Sunday morning, December 7, 1941. This was just a year after my sister Emily's birth. I was nine years old at the time and certainly did not realize the implications of this cataclysmic event. It was not too long before our lives were to change forever. The idyllic childhood years for Wilton and me were drawing to a close. We now turned our faces to the future, confident that our parents would provide and care for us in any circumstance.

The war with all its implications ended the Great Depression. As industry picked up speed to cope with fighting a war on distant shores, men and women were inducted into the armed forces, and folks on the home front strived to support them in every way they could. We children saved tinfoil, rubber, kitchen fat and pieces of metal to turn in at collection depots for the manufacturing of war materials. We saved our pennies and nickels and bought war saving stamps which could be used to purchase a war bond for $18.75, worth $25.00 at maturity.

The first big change for our family came when Dad left home with the truck to help construct Fort Leonard Wood, Missouri, an army staging base. He outfitted the truck with a cot and a tent covering and the means to cook a meal and was gone for two or three weeks at a time. When he returned, he had money to spend. Wilton and I had been given the job of milking our cow and Grandma's cow every morning and evening while he was gone, and for this task we were each paid six dollars a month. Mom also had a little extra money and I remember she ordered a new red dress from the Sears and Roebuck catalogue; quite a special occasion.

Later, when Wilton was ready for high school, Dad and Mom made plans to leave the country. To attend high school, Wilton would have to live away from home, and my parents weren't ready for that. They were also concerned about his social life as a teenager in the country. At first they planned to move to Doniphan, but when that didn't work out, my parents decided to move to Michigan and work in the automobile factories that had been converted into war plants to make military vehicles.

Dad left our country home on April 4, 1944 for Michigan, driving alone. I pleaded, "Oh Dad, *please* let me go with you. I just know you will turn around and come home before school is out and I will never get to travel to Michigan." I was overruled. But, of course, I did get to go to Michigan and, what's more, I got to ride on a train for the very first time, an exciting experience for a naïve country kid. We left from Poplar Bluff and changed trains in St. Louis for Detroit. I was never to see my childhood home again, it burned that summer, the fire set, we believe, by a mentally ill neighbor, who spent a good portion of her life in a mental institution but happened to be home that summer.

Previously, not realizing what a halcyon childhood I had, I often dreamed of adventure and exploration of great unknown urban landscapes; going shopping anytime I wanted, attending movies, having lots of friends and attending a large school where extracurricular activities would keep me entertained. So when we moved to Detroit, I believed my dreams had all come true. It was some years before I realized what a unique and blessed childhood I had experienced in the fields and woods of the Missouri Ozarks. Detroit was to be the first stop on a lifetime of traveling and seeing new sights and experiencing new adventures.

Uncle John and Aunt Ruth who lived in a suburb of Detroit and had told my parents about the availably of good jobs were gracious to let our family of five stay with them until we found a place. This was no small feat since the influx into the cities of people ready to help out in the war effort caused housing to be practically nonexistent.

For several weeks they made their basement into makeshift quarters for us. Uncle John was never the most congenial person in the world, but he was able to tolerate our presence with a minimum of complaining.

Finally, my parents found a little attic flat and we moved in the middle of the hottest part of the year.

Our new home was a tiny four room upstairs flat in an old house about four blocks from Aunt Ruth and Uncle John's house. It had two tiny bedrooms and a little slant-ceiling kitchen. The most distinguishing thing in the place was an old dinosaur of an ice box that required a new block of ice every two or three days.

I especially remember one night when the air was so oppressive and close I found it difficult to breathe. It had rained earlier in the day but the raindrops didn't cool off the air, it simply made the humidity worse. Humidity was high in Michigan that summer; probably every summer, but we were new to that climate. As night fell, the cicadas kept up their incessant noise and the heat didn't diminish. It was a weeknight and folks in neighboring houses began to turn out the lights and go to bed early. Darkness enveloped the community like a black cloud before a storm. We may have been in a blackout for war safety, but I don't remember. Our family was no exception; we also went to bed early. The household quieted down but soon we were all tossing and turning in our beds, trying to find a breath of air so we could relax and sleep. Finally, after an hour or two of misery, my parents got up and announced to us all, "Take the sheets off your beds and let's go down to the back garden and sleep on the grass. Maybe there will be a little breeze down there."

We all grabbed our sheets and tumbled down the stairs to spread our sheets on the grass. *This should be fun,* I thought, *sleeping under the moon and stars.* But you can guess what happened next. We all began to be attacked by the biggest mosquitoes north of the Mason-Dixon Line. Buzzing around my head, before landing on a vulnerable spot, they sounded like P-38s. It was impossible to sleep. Finally I tried covering myself with the sheet. That helped some, but the whole night was a lesson in misery.

Why do I remember that event so clearly? Other nights must have been hot and uncomfortable, but memory fails me as to how we survived them. But you can be sure we never again tried sleeping on the grass in Van Dyke, Michigan.

Perhaps the most memorable event while we lived there was one early morning when I was awakened by a newsboy in our residential neighborhood shouting, "Extra, extra, read all about it. Invasion of Europe underway at Normandy, France." It was June 6, 1944, known ever afterward as D Day.

Just before school started that fall we found a large flat in Center Line on Peter Kaltz Avenue, about three miles away as I recall. Dad and Mom bought a household of used furniture and we were much more comfortable there until Dad bought a little house at 8138 State Park, Center Line. It cost all of eight thousand dollars and Dad could hardly bring himself to go that far in debt. It was a small brick bungalow with two bedrooms, living room, kitchen and dinette and one bathroom. A photography darkroom in one corner of the basement became Wilton's bedroom. We lived on State Park until we left for the west in October, 1947.

Dad and Mom both worked, sometimes seven days a week, and Wilton and I were left in charge of Emily after she got old enough to go to kindergarten. I really believe I was much too young for this responsibility and I am afraid I mistreated Emily; I suspect she has terrible memories of this time in her life. She had long, brown curls and if I was exasperated with her, which I recall was often, I pulled those curls as I was brushing them to get her ready for school. Wilton, Emily and I made a triangle of tangled emotions. I was supposedly the principal care-taker of Emily but when she resisted my direction, she would run to Wilton, who would take her side against me.

I also remember watching out the window after school for what seemed like hours every day, looking for my mother to come home from work. I tried to cook some, but with limited products available, especially meat, I think we ate a lot of macaroni and cheese.

On Saturdays it was my job to do the weekly housecleaning, and I remember scrubbing the kitchen floor and back stairs while listening to Rudolph Bing on the radio announce the Metropolitan Opera from New York City and then listening to an actual performance. In this way I learned to love opera and love it to this day. Parenthetically, many years later when Tom heard me humming a snatch of opera asked me, "Mom what are you singing?" I replied, "Wagner's opera Der Valkyre."

"You are not," he argued, "You're singing "Kill the Wabbit" from Bugs Bunny cartoons." That's how Tom learned to love opera!

Tom and I went to see a performance of Der Valkerye years later at Orange County Performing Arts Center. It was to be four hours of solid opera so at the outset we gave ourselves permission to leave at any time. At intermission I bought Tom a Valkyre helmet, horns and all, with a big pigtail hanging down the back. We stayed to the end.

~ ~ ~ ~

I went back to Missouri during the summer of 1945 to spend several weeks with Grandma Lewis at her home in Ripley County. Without a car we were isolated from everything and could only walk here and there. We did have a radio however, and it was listening to the news that we learned an atomic bomb had been dropped on Hiroshima. The result was that eight days later Japan surrendered.

I was thirteen and I remember trying to imagine a bomb so powerful it could destroy a whole city and kill thousands of people. On August 15, 1945 Aunt Zelma drove out from town to get us and our country received official confirmation that the war was over. Church bells rang, sirens went off and cars everywhere were honking horns in celebration. It was a day I shall never forget.

C * H * A * P * T * E * R

* 13 *

MUSIC AND SCHOOL IN MICHIGAN

My musical education really began when my eighth grade music teacher, Reginald Eldred, took an interest in my singing. My class had a music period once a week which was mostly music appreciation but we also had community singing. I guess I sang out loud and clear and attracted his attention.

Mr. Eldred talked to Mom about my taking private vocal lessons. He recommended sending me to the Detroit Institute of Musical Art on Woodward Avenue in downtown Detroit, which necessitated my taking a bus and transferring on two different streetcar lines. From the time I was thirteen until about fifteen I made this weekly trip alone, carrying my music books with me. My vocal teacher was European—Russian I think. I participated in a recital under her tutelage. I didn't learn much in the way of voice production, but I did learn some Italian art songs. All in all, it was a maturing experience. It was certainly a more innocent age, with my parents allowing me to take this trip to downtown Detroit every week. The streetcars went through some ethnic neighborhoods, but I never felt afraid or unsafe.

Due to the maneuvering of Mr. Eldred, I went to International Music Camp at Interlochen, Michigan the summer I was fifteen. We were, at that time, preparing to make our departure for the West.

Interlochen Artist

Professor Earl V. Moore, Director of the School of Music of the University of Michigan, announced that Doris Randel, daughter of Mr. and Mrs. E. F. Randel, has been chosen to be a member of the two-week All-

State School Choir conducted by the University at the National Music Camp, Interlochen, Michigan, from July 20 to August 10, 1947[6]

I sang in the All-State Chorus and had a marvelous experience. A boy named Jerry, a fellow camper, and I got a crush on one another and after we returned home from camp he and a friend came to see me one weekend. He lived in Grand Rapids which was no small distance away. That was an embarrassing experience for me—at my tender age I really didn't know how to treat him or what to do with him for the weekend. Thank goodness for my mother who handled the situation with aplomb.

Wilton and I also sang in the high school choir under Mr. Eldred's direction and we participated in some state-wide choral events that were a thrill to me. One such time we went to Lansing to a competition and sang in a massed choir of 5,000 voices, singing Psalm 100, *Oh Praise Ye the Lord in His Sanctuary*; one of the great spiritual and emotional experiences at that time in my life. Our high school choir also prepared regular recitals and a musical in the springtime. Gilbert and Sullivan's *Pirates of Penzance* was one of them, and a time of great joy, hard work and fun. The leading lady, a senior, didn't have a very high voice, so Mr. Eldred had me, the lowly freshman, stand behind her to belt out the high *Cs* when they came along.

Soon after we settled in our new home, Mom was able to buy a piano for me. I played so much I had a problem with getting my chores done; I wanted to play piano instead. Aunt Zelma showed me the lettering of the piano keys, A through G, and where middle C was located. I also learned the letters on both treble clef and bass clef from a hymnbook and, thereafter, painstakingly learned to play my first hymn. For some reason, Mom was afraid I would only learn to play by ear, and it took some convincing before she believed that I actually could read some music. I subsequently had piano lessons for a year and participated in one recital. The name of my teacher has long since escaped my mind, but she was a young woman who gave lessons in her parent's living room in our town of Center Line. As I recall, she charged one dollar per lesson.

---

[6]   The Detroit News

~ ~ ~ ~

I had a good experience at Busch High School in Center Line from eighth grade through tenth. One morning I left home in a blizzard to walk to school and when I walked down the driveway between our house and the neighbor's house and got to the front sidewalk, the wind literally picked me up and blew me down to the snow-covered ground. I got up and struggled ahead for one-half block or so and then just gave up and went back home. I was sure I would be in trouble with my parents for that, but later found out there was no school that day on account of the blizzard.

Even though I was not allowed to date right away, I was finally given permission to go out with boys to school events such as plays, parties and dances. I remember one occasion when my brother and I went to a party with other high school friends. A game was played, "Spin the bottle," and when the bottle neck pointed to you, a boy took you out of the room and kissed you. It was my first experience at kissing a boy and I was consumed with embarrassment. It was perhaps too much socialization for a thirteen or fourteen year old just out of the country. Even at that early age, my main enjoyment was singing at concerts and musical plays.

I especially remember an occasion when we still lived on Peter Kaltz Street in the upstairs flat. Wilton and I walked over to Lois Mephan's house for a party in her garage. Lois was probably my best girlfriend at that time and she had a record player in her garage where we kids could dance, eat popcorn and have fun. It was a weeknight and Dad had told us to be home at 10:00 o'clock. We didn't start home until a few minutes after ten and we had about five blocks to get home. It was a dark night and there were no street lights, so Wilton and I walked down the middle of the gravel road. We got about half way home when we heard someone walking towards us. "Oh no," I whispered, "it's Dad, coming to get us." We expected the worst. We knew we were in big trouble, causing Dad to get out of bed, get dressed and come looking for us. But to his credit he didn't say a word; just turned around and walked on home with us. We expected to be punished for that infraction, but it never happened. Perhaps Dad realized that the fear of punishment and the realization that we had imposed on his good nature was enough.

~ ~ ~ ~

We lived in the home on State Park until Dad's health really started to deteriorate. He had been laid off at the conclusion of the war, and spent one whole winter at home, feeling sick and depressed. Mom became the principal breadwinner. He decided to buy a lot in the general area and build a house to sell, falling back on his own ingenuity, as in the thirties in Missouri, to make a living. After the house was built and sold, he spent some days in hospital and doctors came to the conclusion that because of his chronic bronchitis, he needed to leave the frigid climate and go to a warm, dry climate. Dad was a smoker. Why didn't the medical profession realize that this was one of the major reasons for his chronic illness? But Dad had always had a longing to go west. He felt it was the land of opportunity, of new beginnings, and his health was a good and valid reason to make this big change in our lives.

C * H * A * P * T * E * R

* 14 *

PIONEERING TO THE WEST

To make the big move west Dad surprised us all by purchasing a twenty-four foot house trailer. I was fifteen, and mortified at the thought of moving, stamped my foot in frustration. "Oh Dad, how humiliating," I whined. "You can't expect the five of us to live in that little house trailer for even a week, much less months."

Dad was all smiles. "Doris Jane, it's brand new and really very nice. The color matches our brand new 1947 Plymouth. You and Emily can sleep on the living room couch, Willie on a cot next to the kitchen and Mom and me in the bedroom. You know we are headed out west and this will be a good, economical way to make the trip from Michigan across the country."

"May I take my stack of sheet music?" (My cousin Julia May Duane, who played the piano professionally, had given me all her old sheet music.) I treasured that music which consisted mostly of popular songs of the time, like *Till the End of Time,* and *Boogie-woogy Bugle Boy.* "I can get another piano, but I will never have enough money to get a good selection of new music." "No, Doris Jane, by the time we get five people and our clothing into that trailer, we won't have any room left. We will have to sell or give away all of our possessions except our clothes."

Willie announced to one and all, "I'm not going. I will stay with some of my friends and finish my senior year of high school in Michigan." Mom took him aside, out of earshot of the rest of the family, and said, "Now Wilton, your Dad needs you to help him drive on this trip. You know he is in poor health." To my brother's credit, he never said another word, but made his own plans to go along." I moaned, "I suppose I'll just have to marry some old cowboy out there in the Wild

West. Will it be Arizona or New Mexico or maybe California? "I will have to make all new friends and, besides, exactly where are we going anyway?"

Early one October morning our new car, pulling our new trailer, pulled away from all that I held dear and headed west with me sobbing in the back seat. Dad was unperturbed. He just sat at the wheel, driving and singing his favorite traveling song:

> "Good-bye! I'm on my way
> To dear old Dublin Bay.
> That's why I'm feeling' gay,
> For oh! I know sweet Mollie O
> My colleen, fair to see,
> Is waiting there for me,
> Her heart with love a bubbling'
> There on Dublin Bay."[7]

Well, *I grumbled crossly to myself,* maybe it will be fun to travel clear across the country, seeing strange new things. I wonder how the pioneers felt as they left the "civilized" United States and struck off across the unchartered west. I know how I feel—just like one of those pioneers.

"Emily," I huffed, "just because you are a little six-year-old, how come you got to bring that ugly-three-foot tall stuffed Easter bunny when I didn't get to bring my stack of sheet music?" By this time my parents must have been sick and tired of hearing my complaining. *I'll show them,* I thought. *Emily will never get to our destination with that despicable, dirty thing.*

As the miles sped by and we reached the Missouri Ozarks, the brilliant fall colors of the oak, hickory and maple trees filled my eyes and soothed my emotions. We stopped to stay overnight with my Dad's sister Aunt Cad, Uncle Butch and their family. Trooping into their house, Emily took her Easter bunny and when no one was looking, I hid the bunny behind a big chair in the living room. The homey smells of Aunt Carrie's fried chicken and mashed potatoes drew us to thoughts of a comforting family dinner.

---

[7]   Murphy, Stanley, 1916, *I'm On My Way to Dublin Bay*

Next morning we loaded up and continued our westward drive. After we had been on the road for a few hours, Emily cried, "Where is my bunny?" Dead silence. I vowed I would never tell. Actually, after all these years, I don't remember when I did finally confess my crime.

As we continued our drive, Dad continued to sing and invent games such as, "See that mountain ahead? Let's guess how many miles until we reach it." Or perhaps he would say, "Let's guess how much further to a place to stay for the night." I never knew whether it was all bravado or whether he was really elated to be moving west. I suspect it was some of both, and I am grateful for those memories. When we arrived in Phoenix, Dad exclaimed: "I am going to get a job shaving palm trees. Looks like it would be fun to shinny up those towering, skinny trunks."

The sad crime of the missing Easter bunny often came back to haunt me years later. Emily's daughters condemned my heartlessness until I finally told them my own sad story of my lost stack of sheet music. I don't think Mom and Dad realized how much I treasured that music. With a bit of foresight the music could have been left with Aunt Ruth and mailed later. The trailer was, of course, quite crowded. I can't imagine, now, where we kept all our clothes. This trailer, as all others in those days, had a tiny kitchen with refrigerator, sink and stove, but no bathroom, so we had to stop at trailer parks where there were bathroom facilities.

After we left Uncle Hershel and Aunt Mayme's house in Oklahoma City, we were "on our own" - no more relatives. I remember thinking, *I now know how the old covered wagon pioneers must have felt when they set off for parts unknown.* Dad was always terribly positive and elated about the adventure, and he helped the rest of us to not be too full of remorse, but to look at the move as an exciting adventure.

We soon drove into, what was for our eyes, brand new country. Vast deserts, burning blue sky and red rock, cactus and wide open spaces. One night we stopped in a sandstorm at Albuquerque, New Mexico. The next day we drove to Alamogordo, New Mexico in Indian country and then to Flagstaff, already blanketed with snow. I thought our destination was Phoenix, Arizona but after we arrived. Dad decided to drive to Tucson—perhaps the climate was drier there. So we ended up in a little trailer park in North Tucson at 613 Delano Street, which consisted of half-dozen trailers, two or three measly little cottages and a wash-house. Sand, dirt and cactus everywhere. As Dad left the car to pay for the space rental, I had a small tantrum. "Mom, *surely* we aren't going to stay in this awful place. Don't you have anything to say about this? There's nothing here but cactus, sand and gila monsters." But we did stay and Wilton and I went off to Amphitheater High School; Wilton was a senior and I was a junior. I was later to know what it was like to enter a new high school in one's senior year.

We joined a little Baptist Church at the end of the street and Dad found work through one of the men of the church. The pastor's wife was pianist and choir director and immediately put us to work. I remember singing "The Holy City" at Easter services that year. I also soloed a lot at high school parties and musical concerts.

Next door to the trailer court lived a nice girl named Margaret Elberson who became my best friend and, later, Wilton's girlfriend. Mom got busy and sewed us some western clothes and Emily was decked out in cowboy boots. I think Dad and Wilton had boots too, but I wasn't about to be caught dead in them. I did however, have to wear western clothes, during western week at school or get put in the "calaboose." Reluctantly I agreed to a denim skirt and plaid blouse.

One day Dad went into a real estate office to check on lots for sale and saw a man at the counter who looked strangely familiar. Finally, Dad said, "Do I know you from somewhere?" The other man replied, "You sure do look familiar, where are you from?"

"I'm Elmer Randel, originally from Missouri."

"Well I'll be darned, I'm Homer Moore."

They had gone to Doniphan High School together and were, in fact, second cousins on the Whitwell side of the family. Homer and his wife Myrtle and their two daughters, Redonda and LaVonne, became our best friends. We were soon having Sunday afternoon picnics in the desert through most of the winter. After having lived in the almost arctic winter climate of Michigan it was an amazing novelty to have an outdoor picnic in the wintertime. We kids roamed around in the cactus while the four grown-ups played pinochle on a picnic table. For some years I had an interest in growing things, but I rapidly came to hate cactus. I think it may have represented the move to the new location. And I took my anger and frustration out on the local flora.

By the time Easter arrived, it was getting unbearably hot in the trailer. There was no air conditioning because we believed it would be bad for Dad's health. So on Easter week we went to Los Angeles, California to visit some of Mom's cousins. Also, one of my high school girlfriends from Michigan, Lois Mephan, had moved to Ontario, California. We drove across the desert through El Centro to San Diego, then headed up the coast. Ice plant, moss rose and bougainvillea were all in bloom along the coast as the brilliant blue ocean washed up on the cool-looking white beaches. Palm trees and Spanish-style houses made the beach towns seem like paradise. After living in the desert for several months, I thought this was the most beautiful sight I had ever seen—blue ocean on our left and banks and banks of flaming color along the highway on our right.

When we arrived in Los Angeles we found our cousins who lived in old 1930s Spanish style bungalows, with white stucco and red tile roofs. It seemed palm and banana trees grew everywhere in the gardens. I thought it was the most beautiful city ever. Anna Bea and Omar Blanchard took us in for the week. Bess Lewis Morris, Anna Bea's mother and the niece of my grandfather James Hale Lewis, lived down the street. There was also Bob and Margie Burns, Anna Bea's sister, and some other cousins, so we were royally entertained all week. We had a wonderful time; we also visited my girlfriend Lois in Ontario, about 40 miles east of Los Angeles. We then headed back towards Tucson, all of us except Dad grumbling. "Dad, please, please, can't we move to California? It's so beautiful and not hot and desolate like Arizona with all the blowing sand and cactus."

Back in Tucson, the weather rapidly turned from hot to torrid, over 100 degrees every day and no way to get relief. I remember feeling nauseous from the heat. Homer and Myrtle had decided to move to Albuquerque and Dad really wanted to move there also, but for once the rest of the family prevailed and we made plans to move to California. Joy! With no regrets on my part, we pulled away from Tucson and headed west.

Our first stop with the trailer was a park in Ontario, not far from Lois Mephan's house. But Dad was skeptical of this location because of the morning coastal fog that rolled in early in the day, so just before school started in September, we moved to Riverside. This was to be

Mom and Dad's home until they died, more than forty years later. Wilton joined the Navy from there and was, for a short time, stationed at San Diego, learning electronics, telephone systems, and operating the moving picture projector on ship.

I was so happy to be in California I really didn't care where we settled. It was rather scary to be starting off in a new school with no friends or acquaintances, but we were a close family and I felt secure and cared for.

C*H*A*P*T*E*R

* 15 *

**SCHOOL IN CALIFORNIA; MEETING DICK GRACE,
MY FUTURE**

It was my first day of school at Poly High School. I was sixteen years old, a senior, and I didn't know a soul. I rode the school bus from Highgrove to school and registered, got my books and started the day. Walking up to the classics building to attend my first class, I saw several boys hanging around the doorway, checking out everyone who climbed the steps to the building. Wolf whistles erupted and, since I was essentially shy, I ducked my head and kept going. Next day, the whole scenario was repeated but one voice called out, "Hi Doris." Puzzled, I continued walking. How did that guy know my name? Since I didn't know anyone I couldn't imagine how someone could have found out anything about me. On the third day, I stopped after the "Hi Doris" greeting, looked at the guy, and asked, "How do you know my name?" I don't remember his answer, but he later told me he had gone to the admittance office and charmed the clerk into getting my name. He also told me much later that on the first day he commented to his best friend, Verle Sorgen, "I am going to marry that girl." Dick soon edged out most other suitors because his parents were generous with the family car and he was able to get a promise of the car weeks before an event, which essentially closed out other suitors who had to plead for the family car at the last minute.

Dick was a tall, slender, handsome guy, blonde hair and blue eyes, always neatly dressed. Perhaps his ears were his most noticeable feature. They were large and his face was so slim that they seemed to stick out from his head. This impression faded as he matured. He never met a stranger; he was a social person with lots of friends and into a myriad of activities such as Lettermen's Club, DeMolay, ROTC and playing clarinet in the band. He was an average student but tenacious to the max which stood him in good stead in higher education.

He may have been attracted to me out the outset, but that wasn't true with me. Even though I went everywhere with him due to his early invitations, I refused to go steady but tried to leave my time open for other possible invitations. My mother really liked him because of his impeccable manners and social aptitude and told me several times, "That Dick Grace is a nice boy, and so considerate. That goes a long way." In later years I would sometimes say, "Mom chose my future husband."

I was not informed in advance, but was elated to see in the graduation program that I was to graduate with honors, being in the Top 22 of a 500 plus graduating class. On graduation night Dick and I went to Hollywood to the Coconut Grove for dinner and dancing with some other couples. It was a posh nightclub and a landmark Hollywood entertainment spot in those days. Man and woman of the world, we thought. Then, by prior arrangement, we slept the rest of the night in the living room of cousins Anna Bea and Omar Blanchard.

I guess I have to say that I don't remember when I actually fell in love with him. But who could resist such a sweet, handsome and dear guy? So it happened, and after we graduated from high school, neither of us ever looked at anyone else. After all our years of marriage, I have never once regretted my decision, but know that the Lord was in my choice and I thank and praise Him for this incredible journey of marriage with the right man.

But back to school; that first day was painful for me. I had a brown bag lunch but no place that I could find to eat it, so I went into the girls' bathroom. But after a few days I found friends from the First Baptist Church and made friends in mixed chorus. And Dick was always there for me.

I soon learned that I had almost enough credits to graduate before taking any senior classes, so I began to work half day and attend school half day. I first had a job, recommended by my shorthand teacher, working for an old man named Tetley who sold bail bonds and insurance. I was really glad to quit that one, when, a week or two after school was out, I went to work for California Electric Power Company in the Purchasing Department, as a junior secretary. I worked there for four years, working my way upstairs to the Controller's office. My boss was E. L. Sheppeard, Assistant Auditor. He was a very kind man and one of my nicest bosses ever. His son Charlie was a good friend of Dick's. I'll never forget my first paycheck. I thought I was a rich woman. My first purchases were a new watch for Mom and a new suit for Dad. I do believe that I bought more shoes than Imelda Marcos with my paychecks; they were my weakness. It's a good thing Dad allowed me to purchase the piano. I at least had something lasting to show for my labors. I resigned at Cal Electric when we moved to Berkeley in July, 1953.

Soon after we moved to Riverside, we began attending First Baptist Church. They had a good choir and a wonderful pipe organ and my mother purposely chose this place to worship for my sake. I will be eternally grateful, for it set me in the right direction to learn more about great music of the church. It was there that I really learned about vocal production when I took private voice lessons from my beloved California teacher, Helen Catherwood Strandberg, a young Riverside woman who was the daughter of the pastor of First Baptist Church and director of the choirs at the church. She had success of some renown in musical circles and had won several young artist competitions in the Los Angeles - Hollywood area including a Metropolitan Opera audition. She was a student of a once-famous opera singer, Lottie Lehman. She taught me management of air passages and vocal production that I utilize to this day.

Sometime after graduation we moved to Donald Street in Arlington, sharing a house with the Moore's. Dad and Mom put our trailer in the back yard of this old house, and the Moore's had the house except for one bedroom where Grandma Lewis and I slept. Both families shared one bathroom! One of my best memories of that interlude was the wonderful raised donuts made by Myrtle Moore; melt-in-your-mouth treats. The aroma rising out of the kitchen and permeating our little bedroom was irresistible.

Mom went back to work and Dad bought a small business, manufacturing and selling Spanish roof tiles. I longed for a piano.

"Dad, may I buy a new piano on time payments with my pay checks? I saw a new one at Cheney's Music Store and it costs $595.00."

He lowered the paper he was reading and replied with one word, "No."

I pleaded, "Then may I rent it for ten dollars a month?"

"Well, I guess you can do that."

After six months of rental payments, I again pleaded. "Dad, may I buy the piano; they will deduct sixty dollars from the purchase price, the amount of the rent I have already paid?"

"O.K., go ahead." I have that piano to this day.

After the Moores moved on, we relocated to Everest Street, also in Arlington, where we stayed until we went to the old house at 3209

Mulberry Street in Riverside. It was from that house that I went out as a bride at the ripe old age of eighteen years and eleven months.

My first real job was a heady experience. I had more money than ever before, and after paying my ten percent to the Lord, spent most of it all on clothes and gifts. Mom encouraged me to give my tithe to Aunt Elsie, who had recently arrived in California from Flint, Michigan, a new widow with five children left at home. My special joy was getting Emily little toys and not telling who they were from. I would buy her something and leave it on the front porch with a card, "From your secret pal." As I recall, these were toys I had never had as a child but had wanted, such as a little blue willow china tea set. I would liked to have gone to college, but I really believe it was the naivete of my parents that resulted in my not even applying anywhere. Also, to be perfectly frank, Dad expected me to start earning a living. After all, he had done the same straight out of high school. Mom did get up enough courage to ask Assistant Pastor Cy Reid at church to recommend a college for me and he said: "I would hope that she could go to Westmont." The tuition for that private Christian college was totally out of the question for me. Instead, years later, our daughter Susan fulfilled that aspiration for me. In retrospect, I suppose I could have gone to Riverside Junior College if I had begged hard enough, but I said nothing, but went straight to work like an obedient daughter.

Dick had been in the Naval Reserve and when the Korean War broke he was called into active service, having to leave his studies at Riverside College. He first went to Oakland Naval Hospital and served as a Medical Corpsman and then was put into the Fleet Marine Force and sent to Camp Pendleton preparatory to being sent to Korea as a medic. When he got his orders to Camp Pendleton, we made plans to get married before he was deployed to Korea. We just wanted to snatch every bit of happiness we could before the dire date of his departure to the war zone.

We had a lovely wedding at First Baptist Church; Betty Whisenhunt was my maid of honor and Emily was junior bridesmaid. Mom made her dress and also Grandma Lewis' dress. I got mine at May Company in Los Angeles on a trip there with Dick's mother Sarah. I always felt bad about that—my own mother should have been the one to help me choose it—but Mom never said a word. We chose Betty's dress from a department store in Riverside; it had to be ordered in the correct color. Day after day I checked and the dress hadn't arrived despite the assurances of the sales people that it would definitely be there in time. But the morning of the wedding arrived and there was no dress. So Betty and I had no choice but to go out and find one off a rack. I vowed not to let this upset me and sure enough, it all worked out; we found a nice dress for her in the requisite color of aqua. After our beautiful and perfect wedding was over, I was told that Mom and Dad had each taken a day off work and baked the wedding cake; they then had the baker ice and decorate it. It was beautiful.

The reception was held in the social parlor of the church located in the basement and afterwards we took our wedding party out for a post-reception dinner—Dick's idea. We spent our wedding night at Mission Inn and some fifty-plus years later returned there for an anniversary celebration. We had a little honeymoon at Hotel Del Mar, while Dick reported to Camp Pendleton every morning. He got very little sleep that week; we were out to eat every night in San Diego or environs; played miniature golf, went to Tijuana, took in movies.

We had no home to return to, but stayed at Highland Place with Dick's parents when he was off duty and I stayed with Mom and Dad when he returned to the base. Mom and Dad had made another move to Beechwood Place - right around the corner from Highland Place, so I walked back and forth since I had no car. I wanted our own home so badly and looked around for something but couldn't find anything we could afford. A nice old gentleman at church, Mr. Endemann, heard of my search and told me he had a little apartment he would like me to look at. I went to see it and found it was unfurnished. My heart fell a mile as I told him we had no furniture except for a piano and a cedar chest.

"Never mind," Mr. Endemann assured me, "I have been meaning to furnish this place; I'll do it for you."

In fear and trepidation I asked, "How much for rent?" fearing it would be far beyond my pocketbook.

With a warm smile, he replied, "How much can you afford?"

When I told him $50 a month he said that would be just fine. What a wonderful, charitable man. I was too naive to realize he was exercising Christian charity until much later. It was a studio apartment; two rooms and bath with Murphy bed in the living room and eating area in the kitchen. The address was 3993 Whittier Place, Riverside, and it bordered on White Park in downtown Riverside. The street isn't there any more—houses and street were torn out in the name of progress. We lived there until July, 1953 when we went to Berkeley for Dick to finish his degree at University of California.

During this time I sang in San Bernardino Civic Light Opera productions for two or three years and gave it up because I felt it was interfering with my newly-married life since it was something Dick could not join with me. I sang in several wonderful vintage operettas such as *Student Prince, New Moon, Rosemarie* and *Brigadoon.*

At some time during this period I began to realize that the hand of God was on my life, protecting and guiding us. The first real evidence to me was when Dick got his orders to leave Camp Pendleton. His whole company was sent to the front lines of Korea except him and a couple of other men. Dick was sent to Corona Naval Hospital, about ten miles from home. God obviously had other plans for Dick's life and for mine too. We fought our newly-married adjustment battles at Whittier Place and then, after two years there, when we moved to Berkeley.

C * H * A * P * T * E * R

* 16 *

BERKELEY, SCHOOL AND WORK

To date the best thing to happen in our new marriage came after we left home and hearth in Riverside and went to Berkeley for Dick's last two years at the University of California. Dick went ahead of me and found an apartment in a little old Victorian house at 1920 Bonita Street in Berkeley. I supervised the moving van people and then flew up there. I remember it was July 3, 1953. The apartment was furnished mostly with the landlady's antiques. We had an old rose-colored velvet Victorian sofa in the living room that was pretty uncomfortable and the other pieces of furniture were of comparable vintage. It was three rooms, however, so we had taken a step up to a larger sized home.

I got a job sooner than I wanted. I had hoped to take a little vacation, but when I saw an ad for secretary in the Vice-President's office at the University, I applied for it. I was secretary to Arnold Intorf, one of the Assistants to Vice President James H. Corley, in charge of business affairs of all campuses of the University of California. I was pretty proud of myself to have gotten such a prestigious job where I worked in the company of college graduates. When I attended my first office cocktail party I fed my martini to a potted plant just like in the movies.

Mainly because of the parking problems around the campus, Dick and I walked to school every morning. It was about 1½ miles uphill, so it was good exercise. Part of the walk was through the campus itself. I was enthralled by the beautiful forty and fifty feet tall holly trees; I had never seen holly other than in a small shrub. For years Dick teased me about my being enamored with those holly trees. We saw our first hippies during that time, but it would be the 1960s before they actually came to prominence. We attended parades, football games and went to

San Francisco every chance we got. Among our best friends were Jennie and Harry Monson and Vernagene and Roger Vogelzang; all friends from Riverside.

I made the giant step from being a Baptist to joining the First Presbyterian Church of Berkeley along with Dick of course. It was an evangelical Church and I was comfortable there in spite of my "hardshell Baptist" leanings (Dick's description of my beliefs). We had a bang-up Sunday School class of about eighty-plus young couples like ourselves. We also had some wonderful teachers. One outstanding teacher was Dr. Ralph Byron who later moved to Los Angeles to practice medicine at the City of Hope. He was a wonderful, disciplined Christian man. Dr. Robert Munger was pastor of the church then; a great man of God and the author of a famous sermon "My Heart Christ's Home." We found splendid new friends and treasure some of them to this day. The lessons I learned and sermons I heard at Berkeley First Presbyterian really began to mature my faith.

We also became acquainted with Bob and Marianne Stevens, across-the-street neighbors on Bonita. Marianne was a native-born German. For our first Thanksgiving away from home she invited us to her aunt and uncles' home in Walnut Creek. We were most grateful to have some place to go on that first holiday away from our home town. Our hosts were German and, in the European manner, served us wine before and during the meal. This was a new experience for us, but we partook like a sophisticated couple of the world, or so we thought at the time. We kept touch with Bob and Marianne over the years. We once went to the Colorado River with them to enjoy their speed boat, and during the early years when they lived in Pasadena we often exchanged dinner parties with one another.

It was while we lived in our little apartment on Bonita that our beloved daughter Susan Jane was unintentionally conceived. I had begun to feel tired and weak and generally under the weather. After a week or two, one morning as I gazed out our bedroom window, feeling somewhat nauseous, it suddenly dawned on me that I could be pregnant. We had been married almost three years and were both elated at the prospect of becoming parents. When we announced our wonderful news to the family, my mother sweetly assured me that we would find a way to cope financially and she was right. We never had to take out loans and managed o.k. without my salary until Dick was launched into the criminal justice field. We checked around to find the proper affordable pre-natal care. To our surprise we learned that as a full time student's wife, our baby could be born at the University of California Hospital in San Francisco for a forty dollar fee plus a pint of Dick's blood.

The summer before Susan was born, our name came up on a waiting list to obtain an apartment in University married students' housing in Albany, a suburb of Berkeley, on Gill Court. It was called Veterans' Village and was composed of converted barracks. Pretty primitive, but we liked the price--$28.00 a month including utilities. It had a bedroom and a living room with one corner of the living room used for a kitchen. Dick constructed a divider that was about five feet tall with shelves on the kitchen side, so we had a place to store pots and pans. We bought two pine unfinished chests and Dick stained and varnished them (I think they are still in the family somewhere) and we used our folding card table and chairs for dining. We bought a green frieze hide-a-bed couch and a little rocking chair for the mother-to-be, and that furnished our living room. My beloved piano accompanied us everywhere. The vent in the bathroom opened into a "well" that also received vents from the apartment next door and two apartments above ours, so we could hear everything that went on in three other bathrooms and, of course, they could hear us. We could see the ground from a crack between the boards in the bedroom, but who cared?

It was a great communal living experience. And since all families were students we all existed on a shoestring. I tried to cherish each moment, and to remind myself that in years to come we would recall those times fondly. Thus we enjoyed the moment and tried not to live in the future. Since Dick was receiving some money from the G.I. Bill we probably had more money than a lot of the couples. In fact, the couple upstairs always ran out of money the last week of the month and would charge all kinds of dairy products with the milk man, only to have to redeem themselves the following week. I can remember feeding a pot of beans to them more than once. Ernie and Joanne Rumbaugh; I sure wish we hadn't lost track of them.

In those days it was customary to quit work some weeks before a birth, so I worked until a month before Susan was born. I drove across the Oakland-San Francisco Bay Bridge to the University of California hospital clinic for prenatal care, roaring up those steep hills and hanging onto the steep slopes at stop signals, only to down shift, gun the motor, and sprint off when the light turned green. Also, from our home in Berkeley we walked up the hill to the stadium for football games until the last week or so before Susan's birth. We sat in the student rooting section, so I made myself a white smock with Jennie Lou Monson's direction. All students wore white so we could do card tricks at half-time. Mom made most of my other maternity clothes while working full time herself.

Susan did not appear on the expected date, but arrived two weeks later, prompted after a large dose of castor oil taken one Sunday night. Next morning was my regular trip to the clinic. Since I was having some contractions, Dick went with me. We took my suitcase, hoping against hope that this was the real thing. A young medical student examined me and excused himself to ask advice from the doctor in charge. The word was, "Admit her to the maternity ward!" We were elated. Dick stayed around for awhile but then decided he should go to his job at San Quentin Prison in the admittance and guidance office. When the older men there heard the news, they told Dick to go back to the hospital! Later in the day, I really thought I was making progress when I overheard the doctor out in the hallway tell Dick to go home; the baby would not be born that night. I was devastated. How could I bear any more pain? Eventually, in the very late night, I was taken to delivery room and our precious baby was born about 2:00 A.M. I cannot fully describe the total joy I felt and the euphoria I experienced. Perhaps it was the absence of pain and fear, or perhaps it was the joy of parenthood or both. It was wonderful. The nurses had a telephone number to call for Dick and, after dialing the number, handed the phone to me. "Dick," I trilled... He interrupted me: "Doris? Have you had that baby?"

"Yes, don't you want to come?"

"I'll be right there," he said as he started to hang up the phone.

"Wait," I shouted, "Don't you want to know boy or girl?"

"Oh yes," realizing in his excitement that he had forgotten to ask the most important question.

I replied with tears running down my cheeks, "Susan Jane is here."

Dick had been trying to sleep on Roger and VJ's couch down the street from the hospital where they were living while Roger was in medical school. After our reunion in the wee hours of the morning and his first look at Susan Jane, Dick left to drive back home to Albany. On the way he found a store and bought a box of cigars to pass out to his friends. Then, as he was driving to the Bay Bridge, he realized he had spent all his money on the cigars and didn't have the twenty-five cent toll fee. He stopped at a service station and begged the required money from a kind man who ran the station. You can bet that he returned later that day to repay the nice man for his thoughtfulness.

We were so elated that we had a little girl—Susan Jane. She was just what we had hoped for. My brother Willie and sister-in-law Verna had already produced a baby boy for the Randel family, Gerald Wayne, so we wanted a girl. She was a perfect little one and we brought her home to our little student housing apartment with all the hopes of the future vested in her. We were scared too, due to our inexperience. I've always wondered why God gives children to such amateurs. Mom came to stay for a few days and three weeks after Susan's birth we went home to Riverside for Christmas holidays. Thank God that life has never been the same. For Dick and me parenthood has been a wonderful experience. I can say with all seriousness that I invested my whole life in our three children and have never been sorry.

Meanwhile, I joined the Dames Club, a campus wives' club for married students. It seemed a little condescending to me, as the whole focus was on "putting hubby through" with a granting of a PHT degree at the time of our husbands' graduation. It was, indeed, putting hubby through but I was also a person in my own right. When Dick graduated there was an article in the Oakland Tribune headlined *Campus Wives Study, Have Babies, Get PHT.* The wives who received their "degrees" were listed by their husbands' names, not their own. I guess that was a sign of the times.

Dick's last six months of school passed quickly and before we knew it, we were ready to leave Berkeley and move back to Southern California. He had interviewed all over the west and ended up in Los Angeles at the Department of Justice, Bureau of Alcoholic Beverage Control.

C * H * A * P * T * E * R

* 17 *

Moving Forward After School

February 20, 1957 was a most auspicious day. That's the day our second daughter Debra (Debbie) became another grace note in our lives. The ten months before her arrival we lived in a little four room apartment at 1801 Eleventh Street, in Santa Monica. Then on November 11, 1956 we moved into our first home in Anaheim, at 3309 Glen Holly Drive. Three months later on February 20, 1957 our precious daughter Debbie arrived.

Our little home was really a dream house for us. At that time I thought I wanted to live there the rest of my life. We had no money to furnish it, put in a yard, build fences, or anything, but we had plenty of energy, creativity and wonderful family and friends to help us. We managed to get something on the windows to give us privacy. Mom gave us two lovely Chinese hooked rugs to enhance the hardwood floors. By that time, of course, we had a baby crib, a single bed for Susan and other odds and ends provided by the family. It seemed that we had a lot of Santa Ana winds that year. Each time we had a spate of winds, so much dirt and dust blew in from the surrounding strawberry fields that sometimes we couldn't even see the pattern on the rugs. Uncle Royston's cousin Birdie and her husband, Frank Fowler, who lived in Garden Grove, provided us with enough dichondra cuttings to start a lawn, front and back. Don't you just love that name – Birdie Fowler? Frank enjoyed gardening and also provided lots of shrub cuttings. Dick's mother gave us cuttings from rose bushes for a start on our rose garden. We planted fruit trees in the back yard, and in later years their fallen leaves were the bane of Susan and Debbie's existence. When they became old enough to perform some chores it became their job to rake the leaves.

In those days Anaheim was definitely a country town, but the eventual completion of the Santa Ana Freeway enabled people who worked in Los Angeles, as Dick did, to commute, and it rapidly grew into a bedroom city. When we first moved there, we lived among orange groves, strawberry fields and, not too far away, dairies. When the fog rolled in, we always got the earthy, barnyard smell from the dairies. When the children were restless in the early evenings, Dick would often load them into the car and take them to see the cows.

In anticipation of Debbie's birth, Aunt Peggy and Uncle Royston drove up from Newport Beach to stay with Susan for the event. After they arrived about 11:00 P.M. the evening before, ever the proper hostess, I made a pot of coffee. In a short while Aunt Peggy timidly asked, "Don't you think you should get going?" I replied, "We want to wait until after midnight to get admitted so we won't have to pay for an extra day."

But we were soon headed for St. Joseph's Hospital in Orange. It was about ten miles away, and over the roughest road I had ever experienced, each bump in the road was a painful jolt to my laboring body. I did not have a long labor and was able to watch the birth in a mirror at the foot of the delivery table. Debra Ann Grace born about 5:30 A.M. was a hefty one; 9 lb. 9 oz. After she was big enough to get around, she made a wonderful little playmate for Susan. Uncle Royston called her "Tiger" because <u>nobody</u> was going to get the best of her.

~ ~ ~ ~

Aunt Peg and Royston came up every week to see the kids; ostensibly to buy eggs at a local egg ranch, but actually coming to see the children. In a real sense they became a third set of grandparents. Our children were truly blessed by that relationship. They had a color T.V. at their home in Newport Beach and we would sometimes load the children into the car and drive down for the evening. Aunt Peg always treated us like royalty. When she heard us ring the ship's bell at the door she would jump up and start popping popcorn.

In reality, our children had a privileged place to go to the beach because their home was right on the sand in Newport. We would go down for the day and the children would play in the sand and the ocean. Aunt Peg would feed us like royalty, then after using her indoor-outdoor shower to wash away the sand we would go home from her house all cleaned up. Such a life. Sadly, Uncle Royston contracted cancer and died in 1966 when he was in his 60's. Aunt Peg was never the same after that. We tried to fill some of the void in her life, but she basically didn't care whether she lived or died. She continued to smoke heavily, and died of a stroke in 1972, surely before her time. She was seventy-two.

~ ~ ~ ~

Thomas Randel Grace Makes our Family Complete

Little Tommy came along on November 21, 1961; Susan was seven and Debbie five. We had wanted him for two or three years, before he arrived. During his birth I had the most unusual happening at the hospital—an out of body experience. Dick and the labor room nurse were getting me to the delivery room. The pain killer administered to me to dull the pain caused me to become quite uninhibited and I began yelling at the top of my voice, "I need help, I need help, I need it now." After reaching the delivery room, still yelling, I was floating up above myself at the ceiling, looking down at the scene, and laughing at myself and the ludicrousness of the whole scenario. After running pell-mell down a long hallway the doctor arrived at the delivery room to come to my rescue. The next day a nurse said to me, "Are you the one who needed help last night?" After being so accustomed to girl babies it was hard to believe that we really had a boy. Tommy weighed 9 lb. 14 oz. and was born at Anaheim Memorial Hospital at 5:30 P. M.

After a lot of years we finally started to get on our feet financially. Dick spent only a couple of years with Alcoholic Beverage Control and then transferred to Narcotics Enforcement, still with the California Department of Justice. He had an official vehicle that helped with transportation costs. As I recall, he was paid overtime which also helped us make ends meet. I tried to find odd jobs here and there, but was never really successful. That changed when Tommy was about three or so and I went to work for Western Girl, a temporary agency. My friend Debbie Bray kept the children the days that I went to work.

Meantime, I busied myself with singing in the choir at church and becoming active in the PTA. I was president of the PTA one year, all for the sake of Susan and Debbie. Being room mother was another task that was fun for me and great for the girls. I remember baking lots of cupcakes.

~ ~ ~ ~

GARDEN GROVE FIRST PRESBYTERIAN CHURCH

For almost a year after we moved we were churchless. What with a toddler and a new infant, it seemed too difficult to find a new church home. When we lived in Santa Monica, we had attended Hollywood Presbyterian and heard that several couples from there were attending First Presbyterian of Garden Grove. We did the same and quickly found a church home there. Many of those dear people who became our first friends are still with us. Such longstanding friendships are precious. The young and inexperienced Thomas Gillespie, fresh out of Princeton Seminary was our pastor. Garden Grove First Presbyterian was his first pastorate. Time has proven he had the stuff great men of God are made from. Ten years later when he left Garden Grove he served as senior pastor at Burlingame and then, until he retired, was President of Princeton Theological Seminary. We are terribly proud of him and love him and his wife Barbara very much.

Mervyn Burne was the choir director and I found a secure nitch for myself in that little choir of twenty-five or thirty voices. I hadn't sung any since leaving Riverside and I had really missed it. I sang for ten years in the choir at Garden Grove and became a big fish in a little pond; performing most soprano solos for Christmas and Easter cantatas. I also made a little pen money singing at weddings. Great memories. Dick served on the Session and, along with Bill Susdorf, signed the bank loan to start construction on the lovely new sanctuary. I was ordained a Deacon there and Susan Jane claimed the Lord as her savior and was baptized by Tom Gillespie.

C * H * A * P * T * E * R

* 18 *

Making Changes: San Jose, St. Louis, Santa Ana

Dick's years with the Criminal Justice system were coming to an end. His caseload was quite heavy and arrests made by him and his co-officers often did not result in convictions. Unfortunately some judges turned the offenders back on the streets. Dick became very angry and, as sometimes happens, he became ill with ulcers. After a few days in hospital his doctor advised him to seek other means of employment.

Shortly after we moved to Anaheim, Dick had begun work on his Master's Degree in Public Administration at California State University, Los Angeles. While I was having labor pains with Tommy, I was also typing papers for his final weeks towards this degree. I remember ungraciously telling him that if he <u>ever</u> went back to school for a Ph.D., I would leave home. Foolish me—he did and I didn't.

A call came from San Jose State College Department of Criminal Justice, and Dick drove north in September, 1966 to begin his first teaching experience. I remember taking the call from Chairman Mel Miller and really believing I heard the voice of God for this new move. I remained in Anaheim to sell the house and get packed to move. We found a lovely new home in San Jose and a new chapter of our lives began. We moved in the late fall and started making that house into a home.

Susan entered junior high school and Debbie was in fifth grade. We decided to keep Tommy out of kindergarten that year, he would have barely qualified because of a late November birthday, and we were never sorry. I spent a lot of time with Tommy that year, helping him adjust to a different world. He exhibited signs of fear—such as being afraid to see a balloon float away in the sky or paper blowing away in the wind. Our good friend Ron Griffith, who was a child psychiatrist, diagnosed his problems as complications of uprooting the family to a different location and home. So Tommy and I took a lot of afternoon walks and admired wild flowers and the Santa Cruz mountains behind our house. I vowed not to let him out of my sight until he settled down and became our sweet little happy boy. The faculty at San Jose State was quite friendly and we soon got acquainted with the families of the men who taught with Dick. The chairman of the Department, Mel Miller, and his wife were like a new set of parents to us.

My abiding memory of San Jose is the loneliness we felt for our Southern California friends and family. I actually physically ached for companionship. But those lonely times were profitable too; I took some college classes at night and discovered a deep love for learning. Dick wrote a book with two other criminal justice people and I edited and edited and typed and typed. This was before the advent of computers of course. I sang in a women's choir affiliated with AAUW and, of course, the church choir.

ST. LOUIS FOR A YEAR

In summer of 1968 Dick was offered a post at University of Missouri, St. Louis he couldn't turn down. It was to organize a Department of Criminal Justice, hire lecturers and get it up and running. We rented our San Jose house to friends from Southern California and dear Uncle Woodrow and Aunt Una Lee Randel found us a house in Bridgeton, a suburb of St. Louis, and we headed east for a new experience. I hated to leave our new home in San Jose—it was so beautiful and seemed like a dream come true. The family remembers me scrubbing my way out the front door while I wept and wept. Years later Susan told me she was glad we lived in Missouri for a year. She would otherwise never have known what it was like to live in any place other than California. It was an exceptional experience for me too, because I have a lot of family in St. Louis and Southern Missouri, and I dearly loved being with all that family. We invited St. Louis cousins over for cards and dinner and at almost every opportunity we drove to Doniphan for a weekend with Aunt Zelma, Uncle Zack, Uncle Nace and Aunt Rose. It was paradise for the kids with a fishing pond and horses to ride.

The children enjoyed the winter weather, especially playing in the snow. Tom would go out to play after school and take his aluminum saucer, and slide down a little hill until he wore the snow off it. I would call and tell him it was time to come in. Then I would notice how cold and stiff he was. I thawed him by putting him into a warm bathtub of water. We were definitely novices in cold weather. Neither Dick nor I had ever driven in inclement weather so we had some learning to do. We lived on top of a small hill and it was sometimes pretty tricky to make a left turn onto our street and start uphill at the same time. My most memorable morning was a wintry, icy day. After I dropped Dick off at the airport for a daylong seminar in Chicago, I made my plans to get back home safely. I thought, *I'll remember to turn the wheels in the opposite direction if I start sliding all over the road.* When I returned to our neighborhood, I made the malevolent turn only to find the car sliding all over the place. Did I remember my self-instruction? I simply can't recall, but in the crisis of the moment somehow I got straightened out and made it up to the driveway. I believe it was that morning the school bus slid down the street and slammed into a mailbox. I liked the snow as long as I was on the inside looking out. When we went to cut a Christmas tree for ourselves I got so cold I went to the car, saying: "Pick any tree you want, I can't stand the cold any longer."

Conversely, when summertime came it was so sultry and hot I refused to go outside to watch the traditional July 4th fireworks. It was in the middle of that summer that Willie and Verna and family came to visit. Willie came to attend the National Convention of the Barbershop Quartette organization and we four adults went to the evening show in downtown St. Louis, leaving the cousins to fend for themselves. Lo and behold, a substantial thunder, lightening, wind and rainstorm came up. They heard the tornado warning sirens and headed straight for the basement.

In the middle of the banging and crashing the cousins had to go to the bathroom upstairs. As they were returning to the basement, a thunderous bolt hit, and Gerry, the last one to descend, jumped down the full flight of stairs. To be on the safe side, and having been told that one was safe in a car because of being grounded by the rubber tires, Tommy carefully placed his tennis shoes on the T.V. so lightening wouldn't strike it.

When Dick finished his year at Missouri his job at San Jose State wasn't too firm. Thus, when he heard about the possibility of an

Assistant Professorship at California State University, Los Angeles, he accepted the position and we returned to Orange County.

While we lived in St. Louis I continued taking general education courses at a community college. I discovered I have a valuable trait, an insatiable desire to continue to educate myself. I love to learn.

HOME TO CALIFORNIA

Dick said, "Doris, I want you to fly to California and find us a home. Let's unroll this map and pick a good area. We know we want to locate within easy driving of Trinity Presbyterian Church in Santa Ana." We had become acquainted with Pastor George Munzing and knew him to be a man of God. We were confident that Trinity would be a good church home for our family. So we drew a circle around the location of the church. "Are you sure you want me to make this big decision without you?" I queried timidly.

"I know you can do it, just go stay with your parents in Riverside and drive down to Orange County every morning." It didn't sound too scary at first but when I actually got to California, reality crept in and I hardly knew where to start. But I screwed up my courage and phoned Trinity and got the name of Dottie Brown, a local real estate broker, and she started me out, looking for the right place. We looked at resales for several days to no avail. Then Iris Doiron, an old college friend from Berkeley, took me around. Nothing. Finally, good friends Katie and Cy Griesbaum said, "There is a new development in close proximity to I-5 freeway which would make it convenient for Dick's commute, let's have a look at it." That was it—just the right place. A brand new home at 1521 Sharon Road, Santa Ana, near the intersection of Memory Lane and Bristol was to become our home for the next twenty-one years.

Curiously the real estate agent was reluctant to sell this place to me without my husband's presence. He kept asking me when my husband was coming. Finally, I looked sternly in his face and said, "Listen, I am buying this house. He and I agreed I should do this. He will sign the appropriate papers when they are sent to him." So it was done. I returned to St. Louis and began packing.

During our year in St. Louis; we had acquired two vehicles, a brand new Chevrolet sedan and a little Volkswagen bug. Back in St. Louis, the plan was laid out; I would drive the Chevrolet and Dick would drive the VW. I wasn't at all sure I could tackle such mammoth undertaking and the children were still too young to drive. We hit upon the idea of asking my cousin, Roy Lee Jennings, if he would like to accompany us and share the driving with me. He had just graduated from high school and, with his parent's permission, jumped at the chance to see the Great American West. Roy was a nice young man who had not done a lot of traveling. The van removed our furniture and we spent a week in an apartment hotel while Dick finished up at the University.

Then the big adventure began. On the road, we were able to keep loose contact with one another and made plans in advance where we would stop for the night. Before the age of cell phones, it was not that easy. Roy and I did very well in sharing the drive in the Chevrolet and Dick held forth, usually alone but sometimes with little Tommy, in the Volkswagen. To endure the heat when we reached the deserts of the Southwest, Dick carried an ice chest with cold drinks and, with the windows rolled down, tied a wet bandana around his head while the hot dry wind whistled through the car.

I remember stopping in New Mexico and introducing Roy Lee to his very first Mexican food. Having been raised on a Missouri diet of meat and potatoes he was not an adventurous eater. But he was a good sport as he tried tacos, frijoles and all the trimmings.

Finally, we reached the border of Arizona and California at Needles. The children roused up from their lethargy and started putting on their shoes and socks. We're home! Even though we were still a couple of hours' drive to Riverside, they were more than ready to get there. We called Dick's parents and drove the rest of the way, happy and tired.

~ ~ ~ ~

During our first years in Santa Ana, the children made good adjustments to their new schools and began making friends at school and church. When we joined Trinity United Presbyterian Church it became not only our place of worship but also a community where we found friends and where we served on various boards and committees. Dick began his commute to California State University, Los Angeles in the little Volkswagen. He didn't have to go every day, which was a blessing because of the traffic. As I recall, he taught classes on three days and held office hours one other day. Additionally, his hours were such that he was usually not on the freeway during the heaviest traffic.

MY MUSIC IN ORANGE COUNTY

Soon after our return to California, I joined the Orange County Master Chorale (Anaheim Choraleers in its early years) under the leadership of Dr. Warren Marsh and later Ed Brahms. This was an excellent opportunity for me to indulge my joy of singing and get acquainted with others of like interest. We once journeyed to Phoenix by chartered bus to sing a "show" with Frankie Laine and later, with the choir at Trinity, I sang as back-up to Shirley Jones in a Christmas program at the Center for Performing Arts, Costa Mesa. However, my main emphasis in singing has been at church. I have sung at innumerable weddings, Christmas and Easter concerts and have had the splendid joy of learning much of the world's great Christian classical music.

Almost immediately after our return to California, I joined the choir at Trinity under the direction of Dennis Krause and loved every minute of it. Dennis was a charismatic leader and the choir grew under his direction. When he resigned to accept another position, the choir was devastated. The search began for a new director and I had the privilege of being on the search committee chaired by good friend Tom Moon. Dr. Hanan Yaqub was our choice; a young woman in her early twenties and bursting with talent. Trinity's choir has grown to include more than one hundred people and she has been with us for over twenty-five years. I love singing under her direction. Over the years she has offered us many opportunities to sing the great music of the centuries. It is a real joy and a sincere fulfillment of my heart-felt desire to make music. In 1993 Hanan took about thirty from our choir and an equal number from Claremont Master Chorale (which she was directing at the time) to a massed choir event at Carnegie Hall in New York City over a 4th of July weekend. It was a great thrill of my life to stand on the stage of Carnegie Hall as a performer at that concert. We did a strictly classical program, all in Latin: The Faure Requiem, Mozart's Magnificat, Vivaldi's Magnificat and Haydn's Te Deum. The guest conductor of renown was John Rutter, a famous English choral composer-conductor. Hanan directed a portion of the concert and she was afforded her own dressing room and her name in lights on the theater marquee. I could not have been more proud if it had been my own name. We made a repeat trip to Carnegie Hall a few years later and my sister Emily got to go with us. We managed to arrange ourselves so that we were standing side by side on the stage—she singing first alto and me singing second soprano. That is a precious memory.

In 1994, Hanan taught a select group of about forty singers the *Bach B Minor Mass,* perhaps one of the world's greatest choral works. We worked from February to October, studying many Saturdays and evenings separate from the regular choir rehearsals. It is a difficult work and the II Soprano part, which I sing, was mostly harmony, and much like a high Alto part. The work contains many coloratura runs, which stretches an older voice like mine to the limit. But I loved it and it was inwardly rewarding to accomplish this wonderful, major piece.

~ ~ ~ ~

Bible Study Fellowship

When we first returned to California, my good friend Ruth Ralls invited me to attend a weekday Bible study with her. During the years we were gone from Orange County I had been longing for friendship in the church. So that day sitting in that church sanctuary tears fell as I listened to a lecture from God's Word. At that moment I had a heart-felt sense that I truly returned home. I needed the study of God's word, I needed the fellowship and love of other Christian women and this was it.

During the first months, I drove to Magnolia Baptist Church in Anaheim for those meetings, but then a new class was started at our home church, Trinity. I was elated. Soon thereafter I was asked to be a discussion leader of about ten or fifteen women every week. That led into my being the business administrator for this class of 450 women. I felt God had trained me for this position; I loved it and found I had a talent for the job. I worked in this ministry for eleven years and had a wonderful time studying God's word. It was through this study that God changed my life. I learned that every event, every day of my life needs to be filled with God's presence. Betty Matthews was the teaching leader for most of those years and she became my best friend.

C * H * A * P * T * E * R

* 19 *

SAMOA

In October, 1971, I accompanied Dick when he was a featured speaker at an international drug conference in Hawaii. At the conclusion of this business trip I had one of the great adventures of my life. Since my sister Emily and her family were living in American Samoa where her husband Ron taught marine biology, Dick agreed I should go to that exotic little island for a visit.

In fear and trepidation I boarded a plane from Honolulu and headed west and began to fly hour after hour out over the vast reaches of the Pacific Ocean. Looking at a map of the Pacific Ocean, Samoa was barely a pin-prick in the vast expanse. It seemed almost a miracle these tiny islands could be found in a world of nothing but sea and sky. The plane was filled with native Samoans who are big people, both in height and weight. Many of the men wore a wrap-around skirt reaching to mid-calf called lava-lavas. From a lifetime of going barefoot I noticed their feet were thick with callouses and their toes were splayed.

Being close to the equator daylight is from 6:00 A.M. to 6:00 P.M. There is virtually no twilight and night falls quickly. Since my plane arrived about 7:00 P.M. I wasn't to see any of the glorious scenery until the following morning. Nieces Amy, Alison and Mandy woke me early the next day. As we lowered the sails on the windows, we had an audience of Samoan children, giggling and curious but friendly, wanting to have a glimpse of another Palangi, a foreigner. "Aunt Doris, look at the teenager Samoan boy peeking at you from around the corner," exclaimed five year old Alison. Sure enough, a grinning, gangly boy with golden brown skin, warmed by the sun, curly black hair and a big, toothy grin smiled shyly in at me. The news that a stranger was in the village had traveled fast.

Emily and Ron's house, called a fale, was in a rural village just a few miles from Pago Pago, the main city and harbor. Their government built house was very nice. They had canvas "sails" to raise or lower on the screened windows to let in the breezes. No window glass. Their one air-conditioned room was used primarily to stave off mildew and rust on electronic equipment, books and clothing. Their house backed up to the local high school athletic field and faced the ocean about fifty yards away, where waves broke over a healthy coral reef teeming with all kinds of sea life. They had all the comforts of home—bathroom, laundry facilities and modern kitchen.

Emily and Ron had adjusted nicely into the Samoan island lifestyle and, indeed, their girls seemed more like islanders then Californians. To accommodate the high humidity they wore loose-fitting clothing, loose and open sandals, ate local foods as much as possible, and pursued local hobbies like shell collecting. The little girls know the names of most of the shells. When a new and exotic shell was found they referred to a book on shell valuation. My sister almost looks like a native and is sometimes mistaken for a local. Her hair is dark brown and very thick. Her long wavy tresses hang down her back almost to her waist. When it rains she sometimes goes out to the corner of the house and shampoos her hair in the water pouring off the roof through the downspout. When it rains, it really rains, torrents of water everywhere, every day.

Early that first morning Emily's house girl, Lotu, came in the back door. "I brought some gifts for your sister," she chirped, handing me a beautiful, fragrant bouquet of tropical orchids, plumeria and hibiscus. She also brought a large stalk of bananas to hang near the back door while they ripened. Looking out the windows, I could see the turquoise ocean breaking on the reef out front. Up the hill at the edge of the high school athletic field and on the opposite side of the house, banana, breadfruit and mango trees grew up the hill in profusion. Lotu also pointed out kapok and coconut palms. Plumeria, which we see in Hawaii, grow here as large as trees and bloom in great abandon. The essence of their flowers is heavenly. A warm, aromatic, soft breeze blows off the ocean as the rhythmic sound of the surf breaking against the reef becomes music to the ears.

After a breakfast of banana pancakes Emily said, "Come on, let's go into town and visit the produce market. This way you can see what the islanders have to offer us." I gladly grabbed my purse and we drove along the curving coastal road to Pago Pago, about five miles away. No surprise, bananas won the prize as number one produce item. But I also saw green and ripe coconuts, breadfruit, some conventional vegetables, and papayas, my favorite tropical fruit. My sister makes "potato" salad using breadfruit. It is actually delicious. She has made all kinds of accommodation to living on a south sea island. To celebrate my arrival Emily baked a papaya cake. It was lovely and moist, something like an applesauce cake. Milk and milk products are flown in from New Zealand, the same is true for meat.

Ron has a surprise for me. "I've been lobstering at night in the ocean with my friend George Schipper. We have frozen the catch to have a feast while you're here." That night at dinner, tasting the buttery, rich lobster meat after dipping it in melted butter, I think this is the best lobster I have ever eaten. Before my visit was over, I had feasted on banana cake, pie, cookies, ice cream and pancakes as well as some native dishes.

One of Ron's goals while teaching the Samoan young people is to re-introduce them to fish as a staple food. Heretofore, the Samoans have been so afraid of the ocean, they do not launch boats to get out past the reef to do any serious fishing. Over the generations, fish faded from their main menus and their appetites have been satisfied with volumes of corned beef. This was introduced by early sailors who kept the salt beef in wooden kegs because it would keep on board almost indefinitely. Of course, just outside their homes they had all the exotic tropical fruits available for the picking. They do, of course, eat sea life off the coral reefs, such as raw fish and palolo worms (which deserves more explanation later). If you catch a fish while wading on the reef, just whack it on the sharp coral and eat it on the spot. Corned beef is universally called "peasoupo" by the natives. The story goes that when a Samoan asked a sailor what that food in the keg was, the sailor smartly replied, "Pea soup of course, what else?" While I was there, I was invited to go with Ron's teaching compatriot, George, to make a condolence call on a native Samoan household. Instead of taking flowers, George presented the family with a keg of peasoupo.

School children from a neighboring island have to come to school here and go home by boat every day. "Wow, Emily," I exclaimed, "Just look at that longboat cut through an opening in the reef and head out to open sea." The longboat, with several people rowing like mad, disappeared in a trough of waves, only to appear suspended on the top of the next wave. The reef is solid everywhere except where fresh water from land empties into the ocean, creating an open space in the coral, which will not grow in the fresh water. This makes an opening for islanders to get into the deep ocean, but it looks like a precarious event to me.

The humidity is extremely high here and one moves very slowly. A lot of time is spent in the ocean, keeping cool and hunting for shells. It seems most of the expatriate community have shell collections. I even got into the act, looking for rare ones and getting excited over the exotic ones.

On the evening of my first full day there, I heard a gong being sounded by the roadside. When I asked what it was, Mandy, my pert talkative little three year old niece, said with an inflection in her voice indicating, everyone should know what it means, said "That's the prayer bell, Aunt Doris." At dusk every day an empty oxygen canister is banged and everyone is expected to be off the streets and roads and in one's own home, addressing the Almighty and singing hymns. After about fifteen minutes or so, another sounding of the gong signals the end of prayer time. By this time darkness has fallen like a curtain. If you are caught by the "prayer guards" driving or walking outside on the road, you get scolded. Most of the fales in the village consisted of a thatched roof held up by poles over a concrete or crushed coral floor, each room is divided by furniture placement. All Samoans seem to live this way, open to the world and their neighbors. And, incidentally, it is considered fair game to help yourself to anything you see. After all, it is community property in a real sense of the word. My sister's family has had to closely guard the children's outside toys such as tricycles, scooters, etc. Any toy accidentally left outside at the end of the day could be claimed by any Samoan who took a fancy to them.

Later in the week, as a visitor to his village, I was honored to be invited to the Village Chief's fale one evening for dinner. Emily and Ron accompanied me to his cement floored and open-sided "hurricane fale". The Chief, a slender man with glistening skin and black curly hair, his lava-lava his only item of clothing, had gathered his lesser chiefs and their wives and his sons, to serve our dinner.

"I want you to meet my lovely wife," he said after he was introduced to me. He graciously led me over to his wife as she sat on the floor with daughters-in-law surrounding her and children peeping out from behind skirts. The wife, obviously beloved of her husband, was a mammoth lady, weighing perhaps three hundred-fifty pounds and covered with a tablecloth-sized muu-muu. She is beautiful in his eyes because in this part of the world large sized people are looked upon as being healthy and desirable.

The table was spread with their best delicacies such as corned beef, peasoupo, taro leaf cooked in coconut cream called palusami, bananas, papayas, mangos, pineapple and then the piece-de-resistance, palolo worms. Ron looked across the buffet table at me, "Oh Doris, they are serving us palolo tonight! Remember, I told you about this delicacy the other day." Thankfully Ron had warned me that one of the favorite foods of the Samoans is this bright, kelly-green worm which lives in the coral. When the worms come out to spawn, the Samoans gather them up by the handfuls, eat them on the spot, or freeze them for later enjoyment. With the whole family watching me, I thought, *Oh well, when in Rome,* and bravely helped myself to a spoonful of the palolo, and took my requisite bite while all the tribe looked on. At that moment I artistically lost the rest of the iodine-flavored serving in my napkin Whew! International incident avoided. This horror story has turned out to be one of the best travel stories I have in my arsenal of strange happenings in exotic lands. When I am asked, "What is the strangest food you have ever eaten? Is it french-fried grasshoppers, chocolate beetles?" I usually win that contest with my green palolo worm story.

Later in my visit, I also enjoyed a feast cooked in an "umu." In similar fashion to the Hawaiians, the Samoan young men often cook outdoors in this separate "fale kuka" but on the ground instead of the Hawaiian pit imu. Hot rocks are put down first and then various foods are layered to cook on top. Pork is a big umu item, fish and palusami, the vegetable dish of chopped taro leaves and coconut cream, tasting like creamed spinach only better, goes in. Whole breadfruit and other vegetables are placed in the umu and then covered over with wet banana leaves, sealing in the heat and food. I loved the way they fixed raw fish with lime juice and coconut cream. Something like the Scandinavian pickled herring. Every Samoan has a large machete used to peel and break the coconut,which is then grated and strained with a local fiber. The shredded coconut is then discarded and the resultant liquid creates the rich, fresh coconut cream.

C*H*A*P*T*E*R

* 20 *

TWENTY-FIFTH ANNIVERSARY TRIP TO GREAT BRITAIN

In 1976, twenty-five years after our wedding, we planned a tour of England and Scotland to celebrate our anniversary with Willie and Verna, who had also been married in June, 1951. The first thing we noticed about England from the air was that instead of green fields and hedgerows, we saw lots of brown, dead-looking grass and shrubs, indicating a most unusual condition—drought. But it was nice to experience warm weather when in other trips to England we wore sweaters and jackets in the summertime.

Tony and May Hewison, our good friends we met some years before through the International Police Association, met us at the airport with two vehicles. Their cars are quite a bit smaller than ours and with four people arriving and our luggage too, this was a wise move. We drove straight to their home in Bromley, Kent where Tony's mother had prepared tea and sandwiches for us.

After a restful night, we took the train into metropolitan London, heading first to Trafalger Square, which was inundated with pigeons as usual. Then, walking down Whitehall past the Horse Guards Palace, we were able to watch the changing of the guard there and walked on down to Westminster Square and went into St. Margaret's Church, a smaller church which backs up on Westminster Abbey. St. Margaret's is famous for its stained glass window brought from Spain by Catherine of Aragon when she came to marry Henry VIII's older brother Arthur, who died several months after they were married. She then, of course, married Henry VIII. We could not get into Westminster Abbey because the queen was attending a service there. What to do? Dick said, "Oh, look across the way, there is a line of people at the entrance to Parliament. So we walked over, got into the "queue" and soon found ourselves in the House of Commons. What a lucky accident. We even heard Irish priest, Ian Paisley, an advocate of the fair labor bill for Northern Ireland.

Trooping of the Colour

Our friends at Scotland Yard provided tickets for us to attend the Queen's birthday parade, called Trooping of the Colour. We had seats in the grandstand at the Horse Guards Parade Ground which we later discovered was a prime place, seated with some famous Englishmen and women. Everyone was dressed to the nines. We had previous instructions to wear hat and gloves, suits and ties for the men. Many of the men in our section were dressed in formal morning clothes; top hat and tails. Most ladies were decked out in matching coat, suit and hat. The parade began with four separate bands and seven or eight battalions of guards marching in and forming up on two sides of the parade grounds. Carriages then arrived bearing Queen Mother, Princess Anne, the two youngest princes and other royalty. They went into the Horse Guards Palace and then appeared at an upper balcony. Then came the Queen, riding in side saddle, followed by Prince Philip and Prince Charles. As the bands played *God Save the Queen*, everyone stood. The atmosphere was thick with emotion and we could feel the love and awe of the crowd for their sovereign. The conventional bands and bagpipe bands struck up their music and the various battalions marched around in formation. It was a heady experience for us Americans.

Next day we took two cars and toured Windsor but didn't get into the castle itself because the Queen was in residence as evidenced by her banner flying from atop the battlements. So we walked around the village that hugs up against Windsor's gates and had lunch in Savill Gardens, part of Windsor Great Park. May's sister Lol manages the tearoom there and we enjoyed a cold lunch of sliced ham, tomatoes, hard boiled egg, rolls and butter, prepared especially for us. The spring flowers are in bloom everywhere and the rhododendrons are absolutely gorgeous. Some bushes looked to be thirty to forty feet high.

Lol's son Colin escorted us down a hill and through some thick woods to a pasture called Runnymede, the place of signing of the Magna Carta by King John which granted certain rights to the commoners.

Now, years later, my cousin's daughter has researched the Randel family via internet and tells us that we are descendants of that king. See Appendix A. Incidentally, it is rather amusing to learn that the English believe King John to be their worst king ever.

Next day we rented a car and drove south and east to see Canterbury Cathedral, built in 1100 A.D. The stained glass here is spectacular. The village around the Cathedral suffered much damage in World War II. Continuing down to Dover to view the white cliffs, we ended our day by driving westward along the coast to Brighton where we had reservations at the Queen's Arms Hotel. The Victorian shore resorts along the way appeared to have been there for decades and were somewhat tattered and worn, showing their age. While in Dover we toured the Royal Pavilion built in the early 1800's by Prince Edward. It is supposed to be reminiscent of an Arabian Nights Palace and ivory is used extensively to make tables, palm trees, pillars and lamp stands. Most unusual.

Next stop was Arundel Castle, still along the south coast. It is the home of Duke of Norfolk, the most important Duke of the peerage. The castle is set high on a hill with turrets and battlements, with a small village on all sides below. The state apartments are open to the public and these rooms display many famous portraits by Van Dyke, Gainsborough and Sergeant. Catherine Howard, one of Henry VIII wives, was a daughter of this family and her portrait is in a prominent place.

After ferrying across to Isle of Wight, we enjoyed seeing the tall, narrow houses along the shore, many of which were bed and breakfast inns. We found a nice one for the night and settled in. Since we have only one full day on Wight, we started off early by bus next morning to see this popular summer resort. We toured Osborne House, Queen Victoria's summer palace, styled as an Italian Villa and about 125 years old. She died here amid her treasures, many from India where she was Queen Regent during the years of England's reign. Another interesting stop on Isle of Wight was the picturesque little village of Godshill where the houses all have thatched roofs.

Other adventures on our travels in England: Beaulieu Castle and Antique Car Museum, Stonehenge, village of Wilton, onward to Dorset, then Barnstable. We stopped at a roadside farmhouse , 13th century according to their sign, advertising "cream tea." What was that? In this case, it was tea served with scones, strawberry jam and Devonshire cream—thick cream and rich as soft butter. We made our way along until we reached the entrance of Dartmoor National Park; the lower elevations being woods and streams and then higher up becoming desolate with heather, bracken, peat bogs and granite tors. There are many sheep and horses grazing on the open range. The weather cooperated by becoming quite cool and rainy, windy and foreboding, just like a Victorian novel.

Traveling on, we stopped at Glastonbury Abbey, the supposed burial place of King Arthur. Bath was our next point of interest. After some extended time finding a place of abode, we settled in and then went into town to dine underground in a converted sewer at an Italian restaurant called La Pentola. We toured the Roman Baths built in the first century over hot springs. After the Roman Empire fell, the baths were abandoned and eventually lost to history until about 100 years ago when street workers, while digging, found them once again.

We toured Blenheim Palace, the birthplace of Winston Churchill, and then drove on into the Cotswolds Hills, wending our way from village to village and admiring wooly sheep on beautiful green hillsides. Every tourist has to visit Stratford-upon-Avon and we were no different. It is a delightful tourist stop with lots of shops, good restaurants and places of interest such as Ann Hathaway's cottage.

Wales is next. We saw only the northern tip, Caernarvon Castle, where Dick, Verna and I toured yet another castle, in this case mostly a ruin. Willie rebelled. He had had enough castles, thank you very much, and spent his time in Caernarvon at a pub.

We then set our sights for Scotland, driving up the western coast of England and making it to Blair Drummond Farm in Stirling for the night. We arrived about 6:00 P.M. and Mrs. Inglass, our hostess, absolutely insisted on serving us tea before we drove on into Stirling for dinner. She wheeled in a tea cart loaded with tea, coffee and "bisquets." Our soft and comfy beds that night included a hot water bottle at our feet and the lowing of cattle outside most of the twilight night. Next day we drove north again, admiring the prolific rhododendrons in full bloom, heather and Scotch broom. We traveled up into the Grampion Mountains, along several lochs and stopped at Pitlockery for lunch. This is salmon country. We toured Blair Atholl Castle which contained

175 sets of antlers mounted on every available wall space. With us once again in castle gazing, Willie counted them.

Back south, we stopped for the night at Perth on the Forth of Tay, about forty miles north of Edinburgh. It is our 25th anniversary, and we treated ourselves to a first class hotel for the night with a lovely dinner included. Scone Palace is just outside of Perth on an absolutely beautiful estate. Outside the drawing room is a great sycamore planted by Mary Queen of Scots' father 500 years ago. Scone Palace was the site of coronation of Scottish Kings before Scotland became part of England. They were crowned on the "Stone of Scone" which now occupies a place of honor in Westminster Abbey.

Edinburgh was next place to visit. It was, of course, jammed with people and traffic. We were unable to visit Holyrood Castle because it was reserved for the Queen's visit later in the week so we proceeded on to search for Hadrian's Wall, built in 125 A.D. to separate England from the fierce Picts. No luck. We stopped for the night in a Corbridge village and after asking around, were able to find part of Hadrian's Wall the next day. Over the years, this search has become a family joke between us two couples and every time the name Hadrian is mentioned, we only have to glare at one another and make a droll face.

York is famous for their cathedral and we all agreed that it was the most beautiful to date. We had the awesome privilege of hearing the massive organ play and I discovered nine 60 foot pipes resting on the cathedral floor and soaring way up into the gothic arches. Amazing.

Our Lincoln stop was at the lovely home of the Lawrence Byfords, friends from previous police visits. Dinner in the lovely old White Hart Inn across from the Lincoln Cathedral was a lovely way to end the day.

Brenda and Michael Ferrall next hosted us in Nottingham. We have had them more than once in California for visits and enjoy them immensely. As their guests, we saw Nottingham Castle and the Trip to Jerusalem Inn built in 1158, so named because it housed pilgrims on their journeys to the Crusades.

Back south again, we returned to Windsor and found that the state apartments are open. We are treated to much grandeur in the fifteen public rooms. The dining room table looks like it would seat 75 people. Incredible.

Hampton Court Palace, home of Henry VIII at one time, was a gift to the king from Cardinal Wolsey. This place is a wonderful visit for any tourist with dozens of public rooms on display, a maze in the garden where one can have fun getting lost and have an opportunity to learn more British history. For instance, it was the location of the writing of the King James Version of the Bible.

Back to London we encountered a real heat wave. No air conditioning anywhere of course and a major scarcity of ice for cold drinks. We got a hotel named Rubens Hotel, right across the street from Buckingham Palace Mews where we tended to our over-wrought stomachs and got some good rest. David Powis, Dick's Scotland Yard friend, insisted on loaning us his chauffeured car next day so we went shopping in style to Harrods and to the silver vaults where we chose our beautiful silver tea set as a 25th anniversary gift to ourselves.

When we arrived home from our memorable time in England, our children presented us with their portrait.

C * H * A * P * T * E * R

* 21 *

INTERNATIONAL TRIPS

"A journey is a person in itself; no two are alike."[8]

Through Dick's ingenuity, we started to travel the world. Beginning in 1972, he began organizing and leading student tours to other countries to study their justice systems. This was under the auspices of California State University, Los Angeles whereby the students could take the course for credit. Post graduate credit was also allowed and because of this we met many couples our age who traveled with us over a period of twenty-five years. Many became our good friends. In the process of these travels we met people we enjoyed and many subsequently came to visit us in California. We were hosted at American Embassies in more than a few countries such as Australia, Norway, Jordan, Austria, France and Egypt.

Dick arranged with police agencies and courts in the countries to be visited to hold seminars and panel discussions, tours through prisons and educational institutions. One unique experience was the time we met with professors at the University of Moscow in a mutual exchange.

Working together, Dick and I selected airlines, hotels and local guides. For about twenty-five years, we traveled the world, eventually visiting about seventy-five countries. We took the children to Europe the summer of 1974 and the day to day adventures of that trip are recorded in Dick's biography which I published in 2006. I recorded our trips by travel journal, which I kept every year on tour. It's fun to

---

[8] Travels With Charley by John Steinbeck

check back in some of the journals to refresh our memories and enjoy the experiences all over again.

We also began to host people from other countries. Some of them were missionaries who came to speak at church and many were members of the International Police Association which has an exchange program, bringing foreign police people to this country and providing connections hosts in other countries for Americans. We made some fast friendships this way and have kept touch over many years. Tony and May Hewison, police friends from the London area, have been fast friends and we also value Michael and Brenda Farrell from Nottingham.

~ ~ ~ ~

TRIPS WITH A PURPOSE

Because of his experience in leading the study tours for Cal State University, Los Angeles Dick was asked by the Presbytery of Los Ranchos to start a short-term mission trip project. His first trip was in 1990 to Miraj, India. The group that accompanied him came from the Presbytery located in Southern Los Angeles County and Orange County. I remember how up tight I was when he left to travel around the world to Miraj, India which was about three or four hundred miles south of Bombay.

Miraj has both a Presbyterian general hospital and a leprosy hospital. The hospital compound has a nice motel-like housing facility with a resident cook. The group that Dick took worked on building simple housing duplexes for post-leprosy patients. Because of the stigma of their disease, and because the disease left visible effects on their bodies, these patients were ostracized couldn't go back to their home villages.

The following year when another group went to the same place, I was able to go with Dick. My sister and brother-in-law Emily and Ron Needham also went and Gary was along as the pastor leader. Following is a synopsis of this memorable trip.

A Mission in India:

Tropical birdsong awakened Dick and me, as we slowly opened our eyes and looked at the spacious room around our mosquito-netted beds. In the early morning, the stone-floored room at Fletcher Hall, a housing facility for visitors to Wanless Hospital and Richardson Leprosy Hospital, was cool with fans turning lazily from the ceiling. Outside our window, we could see tropical foliage. Were we in Hawaii, or perhaps Samoa or Fiji? No, this was Miraj, India, and we had arrived the evening before by train from Bombay with the Los Ranchos Presbytery Ambassador Team to experience a mission trip. Our task at the Richardson Leprosy Hospital was to build simple housing duplexes for leprosy victims.

The next two weeks were to prove life-changing for us and our fellow travelers. We had come to help others, but were blessed by the gentle, kind and loving people we met. There was no luxury here. On every hand we found much emotion-wrenching poverty. It was the "Monsoon Season" in southwestern India, but we were at an altitude of 2,500 feet and though we experienced humidity, we did not suffer from the heat and, in fact, we enjoyed the daily rain showers.

We fell in love with the people we met, not only the Christians who administer and work in the hospital but also the local construction workers with whom we labored daily. These Indians are a sweet-spirited people, gentle and happy in spite of their circumstances. Collectively we fell in love with the children. Just like home, the boys were boisterous and the little girls captured our hearts with their beautiful smiles and the songs and games they shared with us. One little girl, Surika, about eight years old, captivated us with her big brown laughing eyes, thick brown braids and winning personality. She was always on the front row when the children sang for us. Joy of living oozed out of every pore. She lived in the "leprosy slum" with her family. When we learned that for a reasonable cost we could give a child like this a better chance in life by sending her away to boarding school for a year's schooling, one team member quickly provided that opportunity for her. Subsequently, many of us gladly committed to send other children.

We spent a good share of our days painting, carrying bricks, rocks, sand and gravel. But we also had time to learn about Richardson Leprosy Hospital. Here patients stay an average of one to one and one-half years for treatment, surgery and rehabilitation. Leprosy, also called Hansen's disease, is curable nowadays. Richardson Hospital has a community health program that goes to outlying villages and screens young and old alike for signs of leprosy. We had an opportunity to travel with the community health teams to see how the rural people live in their villages.

India is an extremely needy country and our hearts were moved to compassion as we ached to improve conditions for them. What did we accomplish? We built one duplex cottage and finished three others so that citizens of the leprosy slum located next to Richardson Hospital could have a decent place to live. We interacted in every possible way with the local Christians, hoping to encourage them in their circumstances. We went to chapel every morning with the hospital workers and nursing students. Some attended a weeknight Bible study with a circle of doctors and their families. Others attended a baptism for brand new Christians. But all of us were deeply moved by our experience and realized that we certainly needed to grow in compassion, wisdom and love for others.

~ ~ ~ ~ ~

LIMURU, KENYA:

The next destination for the Los Ranchos short-term mission trips was to Limuru, Kenya. Limuru is a suburb of Nairobi and about twenty miles out of the city. Dick went several times and I was privileged to go three times. We learned to love these Kenyan Christians and made life-long friendships. The work program there was varied. We assisted in the building of a two-story building to house teachers and we worked at providing water wells for potable drinking water for these rural people. One year we ran a Bible school for about one hundred school children. We stayed in a nice hotel in Nairobi, Serena Hotel, and traveled each day by vanloads to the work site. To honor Dick they have named him "Mutonyi", which means the pioneer, or the first one to come. They subsequently named me "Nyakio" which means industrious one.

In addition to the good work we did for the Kenyans, we had some leisure time to enjoy Kenya. We flew to the Maasi Mara Game Park for two days and saw all the wild animals in their natural habitat. There is no substitute for this thrill. The Serena Hotel at Maasi Mara was five star so we had all the comforts of home. The Serena vans took us out on game drives where we saw elephants, hippos, wart hogs, lions, vultures, giraffe—the whole nine yards. There are no roads, so we drove through tall grass and forded streams when necessary. This was such an adventure.

We flew on El Al Airlines, going and returning through Israel, and got a quick glimpse of the Holy Land as well. The short time we spent in Israel was well spent. We saw Jerusalem, Bethlehem, the Dead Sea, Masada, Jericho and the Sea of Galilee. If I live to be a hundred, I will never experience more touching and unforgettable experiences as these trips.

Recently the Kenyans made a trip to California and, on an evening to say farewell to these friends, Dick and I were specially honored for our pioneering work in starting the Los Ranchos – Limuru partnership. Who could ask for a greater blessing than this? To travel, and meet other Christians half-way around the world, do some good work and to give Californians the opportunity to experience these things was a great blessing. The partnership has expanded to include building medical clinics, sinking water wells and orphanages, to provide homes to children whose parents have died of aids or tribal warfare.

～ ～ ～ ～

The Rev. Bob Cunville is one of our dearest friends. He is on the team of Billy Graham Evangelistic Association and is native East Indian, headquartering in Schillong, India but leading evangelistic programs all over the world. He has come to us many times, flying to Los Angeles and staying a day or two before continuing on elsewhere.

C * H * A * P * T * E * R

* 22 *

BACK TO WORK

Dick and I held a family conference. "Honey, it's time to face the music. The girls will soon be ready for college and our budget can't handle all those extraordinary costs." Dick had always left the family financial dealings to me and I knew it was time to get back to work, at least part time. Sure, I had done the usual Mom things—working at our daughters' schools—PTA president, volunteering at church and community, but "to everything there is a season,"[9] and this was the season for two incomes.

I had worked off and on, part time over the years but I needed to do more than that to stretch the family budget. I got a part time job with Joseph C. Smith at his law office in Garden Grove and then about 1980 I went to work for Howard G. Lubin. I stayed with his office for fifteen years until I retired at 62, enjoying the work and never feeling bored by routine. Howard introduced me to computers, for which I will be forever grateful.

In the beginning years after I returned to work, I worked three days a week and the other two days I had the joy of taking care of Grayson and Janna, Susan and Gary's little ones, while Susan worked part-time. Being so close to them when they were small was a priceless joy that has enabled me to have an active part in their lives. One winter Susan and Gary, Grayson and Janna lived with us after they had sold their home in Orange and were preparing to relocate to Huntington Beach to Gary's pastorate there at Christ Presbyterian Church. One day when little Janna, then about four, was playing with Maria, a neighbor child, she took her upstairs to her bedroom to play. At the head of the stairs, on the carpet, was a Chinese hooked rug we had acquired in

---

[9] Ecclesiastes 3:1 and following

Hong Kong on one of our trips abroad. Janna instructed her friend, "Don't walk on this rug, you have to go around it." Now who had told her that? Grayson loved to climb a good-sized tree in our back yard. When we prepared to sell our home and move into a townhome in Tustin, Grayson pleaded with us from his perch in the tree, "Oh please, Grammie and Grandpa, don't sell this house. I grew up here." He was nine years old.

C*H*A*P*T*E*R

* 23 *

THE FAMILY:

We have had such an adventurous and wonderful life. The children were busy with school, growing up and slowly becoming independent. Susan first left home to complete her bachelor's degree at Westmont College in Santa Barbara. After two years there she returned to Santa Ana and roomed with Wendy Steven, daughter of good friends. They asked one another, "Where are our husbands? Isn't this the next step in our lives—to get married and start families?" They made a special time every week to pray for their husbands to be, asking the Lord to bring them in His time. And they are now both married to pastors. Praise God for answering their prayers so beautifully. Gary Watkins, Susan's husband, is a gift to our family which we do not take for granted. We have had the inestimable joy of living near them for their entire marriage, and loving their two children, Grayson and Janna; watching them grow into adulthood.

Debra attended Cal State Fullerton, matriculating with honors at entrance. Her heart's desire was to transfer to Redlands University and spend a semester in Salzburg, Austria at their campus there. It became a dream come true for her; she spent a winter semester there, loving every minute. Majoring in German Studies, it was a natural. I remember those $35 and $40 phone calls that connected us with her so far away. That was, of course, before the time of affordable international calling. After her graduation she went with American Airlines for a time as flight attendant and then settled into a computer programmer job at Carter Holly Hale. After a broken engagement, she decided to make a big change in her life and follow her boss to Seattle, to a new job and a new life. She's been there ever since—married for some years to Kris Wilder and having the joy of becoming a mother to Jackson Hale. Her marriage didn't last, but she soldiers on, raising Jackson and working in a vital position at University of Washington Medical Center. We are very proud of her.

When Jackson's birth was imminent, I flew to Seattle to become a grandma again. Jackson Hale Wilder's birth was normal but we almost lost Debra with hemorrhaging after his birth. As the trauma team rushed her into surgery at four A.M. I could only pray, perhaps the most profound prayer of my life, just two words: "Oh God." My prayer was answered. Debra later told me she felt she was dying but was not afraid. She too prayed, "Lord, please provide a good mother for my little baby." When she awoke from the anesthetic, she realized that the Lord had answered her prayer in the very dearest way. She was to be that good mother. After they came home from hospital, I was with the new little family for several weeks as they settled in, with trepidation, to being new parents. I remembered from my first weeks of parenthood how unsure of myself I was and how I needed the experience and reassurance of my own mother.

Our beloved son Tom never married, but after Santa Ana College and Orange Coast College, lived in his own home in Chino for about eighteen years. He had lots of friends—many of them from the time he worked at Disneyland. He had interesting hobbies, lots of them related to music. He began building a pipe organ in our garage when he was still in his teens. He worked for some years for my brother's business, Randel Amusements, which eventually became his cousin

Gerry Randel's business. He then worked for Turner Pipe Organs, a job well suited to his interest in pipe organs and his expertise in fine furniture making. At the last, he was working at his home in Chino, making Disneyana artifacts and selling them at trade shows and E-Bay. Life was not easy for him and his health problems with obesity and diabetes finally took his life. He loved the family with a passion and family events were highlights in his life. We were so shocked when we found him, slumped over his computer, dead at the age of forty-five. Family times since his death have been so hard as we see and feel the empty space among us.

"Blessed are those who mourn, for they shall be comforted." Matthew 5:4

For months after our son Tom's sudden and unexpected death on July 17, 2007, I was unable to do any writing on my life's memoir. But a day came when I felt the desire to get back to this creative portion of me. Not knowing if I could actually express my deep grief without wallowing in self-pity, I sat down at the computer:

Where do these tears come from? At the very thought of him, I can feel the tears swelling unbidden behind my eyes. It is a miracle, these tears. I am told that tears of grief are caustic and should be allowed to come out of the eyes and roll down the cheeks until the episode is finished. In the beginning after Tom's sudden and unexpected death, it was at least an hourly happening. Along with the tears in those first days, came a racking, shivering pain throughout my body. Then gradually only the tears and memories remained. I was unable to write for months because the very thought of trying to express myself fell so short of the reality. But even as I wept, I have been promised that I will again find joy in my life. Only with the blessings of the Lord will this be possible.

Losing Tom has changed our family life forever. But we have taken great comfort in working on making closure for Tom's life that would be a fitting memorial for him. His house in Chino, about forty miles from our home in Tustin, was totally refurbished by Kirk Tarouly, son-in-law Gary's brother in law and a licensed contractor. It was sold about nine months after Tom's death. Gary and Susan and their children had an active—and exhaustive—role in this endeavor. This undertaking was a cathartic, therapeutic act on our part and we did it as a tribute to Tom's memory.

It is a cliché to say that life must go on. But it must and it does, and we have to find our way, relying heavily on our assurance that Tom is with the Lord and relying on our belief in the Lord Jesus Christ and His love for us. I believe that it will be a journey that will not end, but we are told that, with time, the pain will ease and we will, again, find joy. We attended a thirteen week class entitled "Grief Share" where we watched film clips from counselors, pastors and others who have walked where we are walking. We have given ourselves permission to weep. Music, being implanted deep within me, causes tears to flow. Memories come springing unbidden to my mind and emotions many times a day, cause the grief to surface.

Our old friend and former pastor, retired as President of Princeton Theological Seminary, Dr. Thomas Gillespie, sent us a note of comfort which I have re-told over and over:

" Many years ago I read one of Bonhoeffer's Letters from Prison written to a friend who had lost a family member to death. I have never forgotten the point he made and I gladly share it with you. He said: "It is not true that the Lord rushes in to fill the empty space created by such loss. Rather, he surrounds it with his love and thus makes it bearable. But he leaves the place empty as a reminder of the Grand Reunion in God's future." My hope is that you will find this true for yourselves."

Keeping busy helps but cannot take the place of the grief process. We have purposefully looked forward, not wanting to be stuck forever in our grief. With that in mind, we planned and took a round trip twelve day cruise from San Diego to the Hawaiian Islands. We had a lovely time, met some nice people, enjoyed gourmet food, watched high, forty foot waves coming down from Alaska and crashing against the ship. We read and rested. Emily and Ron entertained us for a day at Hilo, we walked the streets in Honolulu and accidentally ran into friends from Trinity church, then saw the volcano lava stream falling into the sea off Hawaii.

~ ~ ~ ~

A lovely thing happened to us in the spring of 2008. Dick was notified that he had won a holiday trip anywhere in the world! We perused the brochure furnished with the Globus notification of this gift, and chose a twelve day river cruise on the Danube, from Budapest to the Black Sea. We had never been east of Budapest so this was new country for us—Hungary, Serbia, Bulgaria and Romania. We also discovered that we could fly round trip first/business class, using our frequent flyer miles. This put the icing on the cake. What an unforgettable gift and what a lovely way to let our hurting hearts continue to heal.

~ ~ ~ ~

Being made a grandmother by both our daughters has been a joy that is a totally new experience, encountered later in life. I just loved those little ones from the first time I laid eyes on them, and would give them the world today if it was in my ability to do so. Grayson and Janna lived near us until they left home for college and we have been able to see Jackson, a native of Seattle, several times a year.

Jackson Hale Wilder, twelve years

Grayson and Janna Watkins

AUNT ZELMA HENDERSON:

Aunt Zelma Henderson, my mother's youngest sister, has always been an important person in my life, almost like a second mother. Uncle Zack, her husband, died a tragic death in 1973 after being burned by a water heater explosion and she subsequently spent considerable time with us in California. Her faith and love of the Lord inspired all of us and we knew she was always praying for us. She had trained as a licensed vocational nurse in her mid-years, worked at the Doniphan hospital and in her later years had actually worked as a home health nurse in California, both Riverside and Orange County. Her relationship to our family was very special; we all loved her dearly. She was able to fly to Seattle to participate in Debra and Kris' wedding by reading scripture. In the early years of the new twenty-first century, back at her Missouri home, ill health plagued her and it became obvious that she couldn't remain alone in her little rural home just outside Doniphan. She made plans to move to Louisville, Kentucky to be near her granddaughter Terry Beckham. Emily, Ron and I flew to Missouri to help her begin the moving process. She was so brave in the midst of breaking apart her home. After settling in Louisville she made a couple of trips back to California and spent a good part of one winter here. Her visits were precious but also sometimes frustrating and tedious as advanced years impacted her life. She will always be a part of the history of our family.

C * H * A * P * T * E * R

* 24 *

For years I have stored away bits and pieces of family history. After retirement I began cataloging both Dick's and my family genealogy. We took a few trips to the Midwest, visiting courthouses, cemeteries and genealogical libraries. Please refer to Appendix A for the results of some of my research

Who am I? How do I see myself? The answer is, I am an extremely blessed person. I have known joys, happiness and yes, I am acquainted with grief. From my childhood in the rural Ozark Mountains to the present time in urban Orange County, California, I have been sheltered and cared for by a loving God who has given me a good, productive and meaningful life of which I never could have dreamed.

Our early married years were tough, as we struggled to make ends meet. But I really believe those hard years helped hone my character. I remember sitting on our front lawn when I was pregnant with Debra, pulling weeds out of the dichondra lawn, and crying bitter tears. Next door neighbor Don Neidigh saw me and came over. "What's the matter, Doris?" Embarrassed, I murmured, "Our washer is broken and we don't have the money to get it fixed." Another angel in disguise, he said, "You know, I've been looking for someone to help me out with some book work at my business. Would you be interested in a little part-time work?"

During the years Dick and I were traveling internationally, my mother would often say, "When you were a little girl did you ever dream that you would travel the world as you have?" Of course not. I just wanted to live in the city where I imagined there were more adventurous things to do. But in truth, the simple country life was best.

I was raised in the bosom of a family who made me proud to be a descendant of early Americans, proud and thankful for my family and my country. Why was I born in USA of all places on earth? This country is arguably the most coveted place on the earth where almost anyone would want to live or at least visit. When our family left Michigan to pioneer a new life in California did I ever dream that I would meet and marry a man who has always cherished me and together we have learned to serve the Lord in places He has planted us? I longed to be a mother and I was given two daughters and a son to love, cherish, train and turn loose to see them excel in their own ways and follow their own dreams.

I love music and I have been given the inestimable privilege of singing wonderful works by Bach, Beethoven and Brahms and more contemporary composers like Aaron Copeland and Leonard Bernstein. I have sung my heart out under the most masterful directors in church choir lofts, stadiums, performing art centers and even twice in Carnegie Hall.

I love learning and continue to pursue knowledge. World history, geography, Bible, family genealogy, creative writing—all these are passions of mine. I hope I never become too weary to search for more of these things. I love to read and am not content unless I have reading material at hand. I am an ordinary person who has lived a most extraordinary life. I am blessed .

Appendix A

THE RANDEL FAMILY IN AMERICA
WITH RELATED FAMILIES
HUFSTEDLER, WHITWELL, CURL, SALMON

Quaker Church Records of the Friends' Historical Library at Swarthmore College contain records of our early Randels, spelled variously as Randal, Randle, Randall and Randel. These records are on microfilm, difficult to decipher. Hinshaw Quaker Records are more legible, and have been researched by Lena Jo Glaser.[10] The fact that they were Quakers indicates they very well could have come to America from Northern England where the Quaker faith was founded in the mid-seventeenth century.[11] This locale resonates with me, as a description of the early Quakers describes them as making a virtue of simplicity and hard work and a distrust of foreign elite. In the New World, however, and migrating from their Pennsylvania beginnings, the Randels mingled with others who settled in the mountainous regions of the Appalachians, the fiery Scots-Irish, whose long experience as rebels and outcasts, but also unparalleled skills as frontiersmen and guerilla fighters, produced a cultural identity reflected as acute individualism and dislike of aristocracy, a remarkable ethnic group, profound, but unrecognized in shaping the social, political, and cultural landscape of America from its beginnings through the present day.[12] "James Webb… tells a remarkable story—how the Scots-Irish and their fighting faith in America shaped the great nation we are today. His profound insights deepen our understanding not only of this unique people, but also of America's past and present."[13] Kathryn Randel's daughter, Corinna

---

[10] Lena Jo Glaser, *Hufstedler Family and Allied Families.*
[11] David Hackett Fischer, *Albion's Seed.*
[12] James Webb, *Born Fighting.*
[13] McCain, John, U. S. Senator and 2008 Presidential Candidate

Beckwith, has researched the Internet at length, tracing our Randels way back to Eleanor of Aquitaine who married Henry II Plantagenet in the twelfth century. Formerly Queen of France, she was crowned Queen of England in Westminster Abbey on December 19, 1154. Details of her biography are of public record and a movie entitled *Lion in Winter* is a classic. This information adds to the belief that our Randels were English for many generations, perhaps hundreds of years.

Our Randel forefathers adopted the musical styles of Ireland and Scotland; the jigs and reels and the musical instruments used in producing this music. These tunes are played to this day by old time fiddlers, accompanied by guitar, perhaps piano, and sometimes with rhythmic clacking spoons for percussion. My brother Willie is quite accomplished in this regard, not only playing a skillful old-time fiddle but serving regularly as judge of old time fiddle contests.

Having said all this, regardless of the origin of our Randels, it is a sure thing that they were independent people and, upon migration to America, settled in the Appalachians from Pennsylvania to the deep south. Normal migration patterns, generally east to west, eventually brought our branch of the Randel family from Perry County, Tennessee to Ripley County, Missouri in 1880.

Most of the family was hard-working, middle-class farmers or artisans. But among earlier Randels in our family line also were ministers of the gospel and politicians. One fine example is Riley Randel, who was a member of the Tennessee Legislature in the mid-twentieth century. There is a bridge named in his honor, *Randel Bridge*, at Buffalo River, Linden County, Tennessee. Another line of our Randels has spawned medical doctors in every generation.

Royleta Malone, a cousin from the Whitwell branch, and a family history researcher *par excellence,* wrote a family history of the Randels which was published in 2001. She counts more than 3,000 descendants in ten generations since 1776.

JOSEPH AND ANN RANDEL:

The first Randel in America we can claim as our ancestor is Joseph Randel of Padgetts Creek, S.C. and Bush River, N.C. He would have been born around 1740, probably in Pennsylvania. He married Ann. Their large family of eleven children were:

Sarah	Dec 30, 1763
Joseph	May 29, 1765
Jonas	Dec 4 1766
Isaac	Dec 12, 1768
Thomas	Jan 12, 1771
Ann	Oct 9, 1773
Hannah	Feb 12, 1775
Moses[14]	Oct 30, 1776
John	Nov 10, 1779
Lydia	Dec 4, 1781
Rachel	Dec 27, 1783

Joseph and Ann owned land in Chester County, Pennsylvania 1765-1771 so their older children would have been born there.

MOSES AND REBECCA RANDEL:

Moses was born in Union County, South Carolina and in 1798 married a woman named Rebecca who was born around 1769 in Pennsylvania so she was probably a Quaker also. She died before the 1860 Census in Perry County, Tennessee. Their children were:

Amos	ca 1799 Georgia
John R.	ca 1806 Tennessee
Lucinda	ca 1807 Tennessee
Nathanial Moses	Jan 1, 1809 Kentucky
Frances L.	ca 1808
Jane	ca 1811 Kentucky

Moses and Rebecca moved around a lot. They lived in Franklin County, Georgia; Perry County, Tennessee; Barren County, Kentucky and were found in Little Pigeon Creek, Indiana in 1818-1821. They belonged to the Little Pigeon Creek Baptist Church which tells us that they left the Quaker faith at some point. In Perry County, Tennessee, 1820, Moses received a land grant, Grant No. 1880 on Rockhouse Creek, October 18, 1820. This was on Buffalo River in Range 9,

---

[14] Bold print indicates our direct ancestor

Section 4. By 1860 a large contingent of the Moses Randel family lived in Perry County, Tennessee. However, Jonas and Sarah Randel were found in Preble County, Ohio. Frances had married Shadrack Lewis[15] and Lucinda had married Benjamin Pearson.

Moses and his sons served on juries in early Perry County and they were all quite large land owners and prominent citizens. Quakers did not usually own slaves, but Moses owned at least eleven slaves in 1860, shown in census records; in those days not a small fortune.

JOHN R. RANDEL:

We are fortunate to know more about John R. Randel, Moses' son and our ancestor, because of his Bible record, copied by his son and my great grandfather Nacy Meeks Randel.

John R. Randel was born around 1806 in Tennessee, married around 1828 and died in Perry County, Tennessee in 1873. He married Nancy Markham. John R. and his brother Nathaniel "Nacy" Moses Randel married sisters. John R. married Nancy and Nacy married Mahalia. John R. and Nancy's ten children were all born in Perry County, Tennessee:

Paschal (or Pascham) M.	Oct 9, 1829
Livonia C.	Jan 29, Jan 1831
Amanda E.	June 2, 1832
Angeline A. (Jincy)	Jan 10, 1834
Nacy Meeks	July 5, 1837
Nancy A.	Oct 8, 1839
John C.	Nov 20, 1841
Sarah R.	June 20, 1844
Harriet D.	Dec 1,1849
William A.	Dec 5, 1854

---

[15]   Included in my Lewis family ancestry

NACY MEEKS RANDEL

Nacy was named for his Uncle Nathaniel Moses Randel, whose nickname was Nacy. The origin of his middle name is not known for certain as it appears both as *Meek* and *Meeks* in extant records. However, a Christian Church minister by the name of Rufus Meeks[16] appears in the History of Hickman County, Tennessee. Nacy could have been named for him and, based on that premise, I have chosen to refer to him as Nacy Meeks.

Nacy was born in Linden, Perry County, Tennessee on July 5, 1837. When he was nineteen years old he married Rebecca Carolyn Whitwell, age seventeen. Their children, all born in Perry County, Tennessee, were

Martha E.	Mar 31, 1857
William R.	Jan 23, 1859
Andrew Claborn	Dec 22, 1861
John Thomas Murray	Dec 27, 1864
Willis Amos	Oct 10, 1866
Lewis Austin	Jul 22, 1869
Robert Thomas	Aug 2, 1877

Nacy was a soldier of the Confederacy in the Civil War as a Sergeant in Company B, 10th Cavalry. He labored as a farmer both before and after the Civil War, always making a meager living. He complained of poverty, once being quoted as saying, "When honey drops from heaven my cup is always upside down."

After the Civil War, things were very bad in Tennessee for all Southerners and especially for former Confederates. In some ways Reconstruction from 1865 to1877 was worse than the war itself. Perry Countians were leaving in large numbers to go to other states and Nacy and his family decided to leave also.[17] When Nacy was forty-three and no longer a young man, the family decided to make a big move to Ripley County, Missouri, joining seventeen other families made up of family and friends. The leader of the group was Andrew Jackson Whitwell,

---

16   Jerome D. Spence, *A History of Hickman County, Tennessee*
17   Malone,Royleta C., *Randel Family History, page K.*

Rebecca's brother. Andrew had made a previous trip to Ripley County and bought up a large tract of land in northwestern Ripley County.

Nacy and Rebecca's oldest daughter, Martha, died as a young girl and was buried in Tennessee. The rest of the children joined their parents on the big move to Ripley County, Missouri in 1879-80. The wagon train stopped and camped, resting over one Sunday with Rebecca's brother, Willis Whitwell, who had moved to Stoddard County, Missouri (east of Ripley County) some time earlier. The trip from Hickman County to Ripley County was about 350 miles and it took them fourteen days by wagon.

Others in the wagon train were to be their neighbors and close friends in Ripley County. Some of these families were William and Rebecca Whitwell, John Wesley Hufstedler and Ann Maria Curl Hufstedler, Harvey O. Randel family, William H. Randel family and the Rev. Andrew J. Edwards family.

In Ripley County, Nacy acquired land bordered on the south by Buffalo Creek. This property was part of the much larger tract previously purchased by Andrew Jackson Whitwell. Nacy built a log house, called a dog trot house.[18] The main part of Nacy's house was two stories tall and boasted two handsome chimneys made of brick. The central rooms were 16 feet square. Since Nacy moved to Ripley County in 1880, his home was built sometime after that, and was not far from one hundred years old at the time it burned in May, 1975. One chimney of this house still stands. It is just off the C Road at the turn-off to the community of Bennett.

---

[18]   Pioneer log building had its limitations. The length of any wall was limited by the height of straight tree trunks on the land and the weight of a log that one or two people could lift. It is rare for an old log building to have any walls that are longer than twenty feet. Dogs and their masters found that the open bay, between two long flat walls, acted as a funnel for cooling breezes. When a barn or cabin needed to be larger than twenty feet by twenty feet, pioneers built a series of small rooms and joined them under the same roof. One of the most common arrangements was the dog-trot.

Rebecca Caroline lived only twelve years after their migration to Ripley County, dying on March 11, 1892 at the age of 53. She is buried in Bennett Cemetery.

Nacy Meeks didn't waste much time as a widower; he remarried just four months later on July 17, 1892 to Delila Logan. Nacy was 55 and she was 23. He and Delila had two sons; Robert Guy, born April 19, 1893 and Samuel P. born July 26, 1895. When little Samuel was only three their mother Delila died.

When the children were four and six years old, their father Nacy Meeks married Mary Elizabeth "Betty" Drake Hodo, a widow, on August 30, 1896. Betty maintained a central telephone office in their log house on Buffalo as well as raising the young children left motherless. He and Betty lived together for eighteen years before he died in Ripley County, at the home place, on March 26, 1914. He was seventy-seven and had outlived all of his siblings, two of his wives, and three of his own children. He is buried in Bennett Cemetery.

LEWIS AUSTIN "AUSTIN" RANDEL:

When my grandfather Austin was ten years old, he came to Ripley County with his parents in 1880 when the elder Randels heard of the promise of fertile land in Southern Missouri. These natives were a strong, independent breed, mostly of Scots-Irish and Northern English stock. Thousands of them emigrated to the New World in the 18th century, sailing over the Atlantic to settle in the Appalachian Mountain chain from Pennsylvania to North Carolina. They brought an allegiance to the family or clan rather than to any government, and were ready to fight to preserve their beliefs. Sharpshooting was cultivated among the men and they earned a reputation in the Revolutionary and Civil Wars by changing some of the methods of battle.

Austin vividly remembered his family's migration to Ripley County, Missouri from Perry County, Tennessee. According to his story, they crossed the Mississippi at Thebe's Ferry and shipped everything from there to Poplar Bluff by railroad. They arrived in Ripley County on New Year's Day, 1880.

In 1893, when he was 23, Austin married Ida Hufstedler, daughter of John Wesley Hufstedler and Ann Maria Curl II, and had a family of thirteen children, eight growing to adulthood:

Ollye	Sept 7, 1894
Claude Casey	Apr 21, 1897
Infant daughter	1899
Infant daughter	1900
Robert Thomas	Nov 18, 1900
Caroline May "Cad"	Apr 10, 1903
Elmer Folk	**June 10, 1905**
John Nace	Oct 26, 1907
Grover Cleveland	1909
Infant son	1911
Lewis Woodrow	Nov 1, 1912
Ida Marie	Sep 21, 1914
Helen Frances	Feb 11, 1917

Austin and Ida bought a farm in the Lone Star district but some years later, in January 1919, Austin lost Ida to tuberculosis and the flu epidemic of 1919. Austin was devastated; he hardly knew what to do with the younger children, especially his little toddler daughters. Older sisters, Ollye and Cad, helped out as substitute mothers and somehow they survived, but the younger children remember their sad childhood.

Most of Austin's children taught school when they completed their own education. Robert was a soldier in France in WWI, and the younger siblings worked in the war effort in WWII. Nace served in the South Pacific as a Seabee during World War II. He was caught behind enemy lines on Guadalcanal, surviving only on wormy rice.

My memories of Granddad Randel are rather vague, but I know this much. He must have had a sense of humor because an early picture of the family on the front porch of their Lone Star farm home shows the young family all in Sunday-go-to-meetin' clothes. Ida holds my father Elmer, an infant, on her lap, wearing a dress,[19] and Granddad Randel is sitting primly on his chair, holding a big rooster.

In 1928, Austin married Kate Boster and they had a daughter, Opal Randel Hall, who has lived in Doniphan all her life. In the 1940's Austin sold the farm and bought property at the highway junction in

---

[19]   I have recently learned that putting toddler boys in dresses was a practical move to aid in toiletry issues. This custom was observed in England as well as our country.

West Doniphan. He built a little convenience store at the intersection. He died in 1951 and Kate passed away in 1960.

ELMER FOLK RANDEL

Dad was named for Joseph W. Folk, governor of Missouri at the time of his birth. He didn't like farming and soon found that he wasn't cut out to be a school teacher either, but he did teach school for one year just out of high school and after successfully passing the Missouri state teacher's examination. Later he went to St. Louis and worked in the General Motors plant and, while there, married his high school sweetheart, Edna May Lewis in May of 1929. Their children:

Wilton Lewis, December 12, 1929
Doris Jane, July 8, 1932
Emily Imogene, December 23, 1940

Elmer had a desire to learn electrical engineering and, during those lean years, purchased an encyclopedia of electrical engineering which he studied at great length. Two children were born in St. Louis, Wilton Lewis and Doris Jane, and when the Great Depression made life hard in the big city, they returned to southern Missouri where Edna's father ceded them enough land from the Lewis farm to build a house in the country. Elmer used his electrical knowledge to wire their new house for electricity, building his own electrical plant to provide the power. He was rightfully proud that he never used Federal assistance during the Great Depression, but managed a living by raising chickens on a large scale, pigs, mushrooms and having a country grocery store. He also used his truck to haul railroad ties for other people out of the deep woods to Doniphan.

Elmer was an honest and upright man, respected in the community. He served on the local school board and had more than a few persons paroled to him by the court.

At the onset of World War II Elmer left home to help build Fort Leonard Wood near Columbia, Missouri and, thinking of higher education necessities for their children, moved the family to Detroit, Michigan where Edna and Elmer both worked in the defense factories, sometimes seven days a week.

Elmer's health deteriorated in that harsh climate and doctors recommended that he go to a warm, dry climate. Accordingly, in late fall of 1947 the family moved to Tucson, Arizona where they wintered and then continued to California in the summer of 1948 where they settled in Riverside. Elmer spent the last half of his life, 43 years, as a resident of Riverside. He was initially self-employed but then worked as a carpenter for the Air Force for 19 years. He and Edna were able to enjoy an active retirement life, twenty-five years, by traveling by pickup and camper to all forty-eight states plus Alaska and much of Canada.

He enjoyed hunting and fishing and loved to sing. He learned to read shaped notes as a young man, and enjoyed getting together with his brother Bob and other family members to sing either old-time gospel songs or rounds. All three of his children carry on his love of music. His grandchildren love the songs, rhymes, limericks and rounds he taught them and these memories add to their rich heritage. They are being passed on to the great-grandchildren.

Elmer was not one to vocalize his faith, but he was a firm believer in the Lord Jesus Christ. In later years he enjoyed his daily Bible readings and his self-appointed contribution to the Sunday morning services was to add a resounding "Amen" at the finish of any special music.

THE HUFSTEDLER FAMILY

WITH RELATED FAMILIES
CURL, SALMON, STORY, WATSON, MATHEWS, GAMBLIN

The Hufstedler family has been thoroughly researched by Lena Jo Glaser[20] who published a large volume in 1974, using already published research from previous years and building up a family history with her own copious research. The name Hufstedler has gone through many spellings over the years, such as Hochstettler, Hofstalor, Hoffseaker. They were Swiss by birth and subsequently settled in North Carolina and South Carolina, later making it to Perry County, Tennessee and eventually to Ripley County, Missouri.

The hardships under which they lived, and the many moves they made due to persecution, leaves one filled with awe that they survived. It is not definitely known whether it was the active religious persecution in Switzerland and the Palatinate, or the yearning to be free to own their own land, or both, which prompted them to join with the steady stream of immigrants and cross the Atlantic to America.[21]

In this family we are descended from a fine line of American patriots, soldiers from the Revolutionary War, War of 1812, Civil War, World War I and World War II.

I admit to being proud to have Hufstedler blood in my veins. The many members of that family whom I have met are intelligent, articulate, by and large well-educated, and long-lived. A recent picture at the annual Hufstedler reunion show four elder Hufstedlers, all in their nineties, and looking good.

According to the Glaser book, my grandmother Ida Hufstedler Randel was the fifth generation of "our" Hufstedlers to be in America. They are as follows:

---

20   Glaser, *ibid.*
21   Glaser, ibid.

John Jacob Hufstedler, born 1736, possibly on the Ship Harle bound for America. He married Susannah. Jacob Hufstedler is the only child known.

Jacob Hufstedler 1785 – 1860, married Alcey Moore
> John 1805
> David 1807
> Joseph Freeman 1810
> **James Henry 1813 - 1873**
> Elizabeth "Betsy" 1815
> Pinkney "Pink" 1817
> Samuel Moore 1819
> Susannah "Susan" 1823
> Alcey 1825

James Henry Hufstedler, 1813-1873, married Elizabeth Elder Salmon
> Mary Jane 1836
> Alcey 1837
> **John Wesley   1839 – 1896**
> Martha 1840
> Nancy 1843
> Samuel Moore 1845
> James Clay 1848
> Jacob F. 1850
> Margaret 1853
> William Henry Harrison 1856
> George Washington 1859

John Wesley Hufstedler 1839-1896, married Ann Maria Curl; my great-grandparents.
> Cora 1873
> John Thomas 1875
> **Ida Oct 22, 1877 – Jan 7, 1919**
> Samuel Rufus 1881
> Elizabeth Ann "Bessie" 1885

Frances "Frankie" 1887
George Washington 1889

John Wesley married Sarah "Sack" Stevens:
James Wiley 1448
Jacob William "Willie" 1861
Minnie 1867
David 1870

~ ~ ~ ~

IDA HUFSTEDLER:

My grandmother Ida married Lewis Austin Randel on November 26, 1893 in Ripley County, Missouri. He was twenty-four and she was sixteen.

Since Ida died when my Dad was a young boy, I never had the privilege of personally knowing my maternal grandmother. I have a few pictures and have been told by my Dad's cousin Eva Lena Randel Klenn, who personally remembered her Aunt Ida, that she was a beautiful lady with strawberry red hair, who could sing like an angel and play many musical instruments. She was left-handed just like me. Members of the Hufstedler family felt that Ida had a hard life after she married Austin. She had so many children, thirteen children in a span of twenty-three years, five dying at birth and one little boy, Claude Casey, dying at age six.

In her late thirties she contracted tuberculosis. It was commonly believed in that era that the fresh and clear air of Colorado would heal this disease, so Granddad Randel sent her there to get well. She was on a train coming home preparatory to the whole family moving west when she apparently contracted the 1918-19 flu and could not recover because of her damaged lungs. She died January 7, 1919. The children remember that they had planned to move to Colorado and had the sale fliers all printed to sell the Missouri farm when she died.

THE CURL FAMILY

WILLIAM CURL, SR:

A native of Sussex County, England, William Curl, Sr. married Mary Richardson about 1760 in Chatham, North Carolina. He was a soldier in the Revolutionary War.

WILLIAM CURL, JR:

William Curl, Jr. was a member of the Senate, 14th General Assembly of Tennessee 1821-23, representing Perry, Humphreys and Stewart Counties. He was born in Chatham County, North Carolina in 1767 and lived until the age 94, dying in Hickman County, Tennessee. He married an amazing woman named Kezziah Gamblin, a native of North Carolina. Her father was an officer in the Revolutionary War.[22]

William Curl settled in Hickman County, was principally a farmer but is also listed in records as a saddler. He was made sheriff of Stewart County in 1804; one of the first justices of the peace in Hickman County and a member of the Baptist Church.

When he first settled there the Indians from across the Duck River were frequent visitors at his house. They were at all times friendly. Kezziah, William's wife, was always kind to the Indians and much loved by them. On one of their visits they found her seriously ill. They immediately commenced ceremonies, after the fashion of their tribe, to frighten away the evil spirits.[23] Kezziah was healed and lived to be 107 years old.

William and Kezziah had thirteen children from 1795 to 1817 and raised ten of them. They are as follows:

Jarret, 1795
Mary, 1979
Susan, 1800
Philadelphia "Delphia, 1802

---

22   Goodspeed, *History of Central Arkansas*
23   Spence, *History of Hickman County, Tennessee*

Ruth, 1804
Minerva 1806
Abisha W. Curl, June 7, 1809
Kezziah, 1812
Larkin Jackson, 1814
Martha "Patsy", 1817

ABISHA W. CURL:

This patriot served in the Civil War, a private in Willis Whitwell's Company C, 10th Tennessee Cavalry, Confederate States of America. He was taken prisoner and died at the age of fifty-four of dysentery shortly after being released.

The following children were born of Abisha and Ann Maria I:

William 1837
Sarah Kezziah 1839
Sophronia Adeline "Fronia" 1841
Thomas 1842
John Burton 1845
Ann Maria II, December 27, 1846
Mary Jane 1850
Andrew Jackson 1852
Virginia Elizabeth "Jennie" 1855

His wife, Ann Maria Watson, whom he married on July 21, 1836, received the following letter after his death. It was dated May 24, 1863 from Grand Hospital, Petersburg, Virginia:

Dear madam, by special request of your husband, Mr. Abishai Curl, I assume the privilege of writing a few lines.

Your husband came here a paroled prisoner (captured near Parkers + Roads Tenn.) on the 22nd day of April 1863, with chronic diarrhea, where he remained until God saw fit to remove him from this land of sorrow to a world of bliss. He died this morning at six o'clock, and no man ever breathed his life out sweeter with a full confidence of going to rest. I was with him nearly all the time of his sickness, being his nurse, and he never had one glimmering ray of doubt on his mind.

He wished to get home and see you, and die with his friends, but said, "God is just." Yesterday he tried to sing a hymn, "When we've been there ten thousand years, bright shining as the sun, we've no less days to sing God's praise than when we first begun," but his voice failed him and he had to stop, and told me he was dying for his eyes grew dim. He said, "Joe, I will soon leave you. I want you to write to my wife, she is a mighty good old lady, send her all the money I have and tell her to employ a sharp executor and sell all she can spare to pay for the balance of my land." This is verbatim.

Your husband will be buried nicely and grave marked. I wrote you yesterday, enclosed thirty five dollars. It was by Mr. Curl's direction that I did it. He has left nothing here but a pair of shoes. Your husband was treated kindly, and died among Christian friends of the same faith. Your loss is his eternal gain, so dear lady let me ask you not to mourn after him as those that have no hope. I pray that my last on earth may be like his, for in the hour of death he felt that God was near.

I am unknown but true friend, J. G. Collier

His wife, Ann Maria Watson, knew the true meaning of grief because she not only lost her husband but one son, Thomas, also a Confederate soldier, who died in a prison camp. See short biography of this strong and stalwart woman below:

ANN MARIA WATSON, Wife of Abisha Curl:

Tradition in the Curl family connects the well-known Methodists, The Rev. Samuel Watson, Sr. and the Rev. Samuel Watson, Jr. with the William Watson family.[24]

It has long been a belief in the Hufstedler family that Ann Maria Watson Curl was half Choctaw Indian. Her paternal ancestor, William Curl, Sr., was an Englishman. Her father was William Watson, with connections to the well-known Methodists. So it would have been her mother, Sarah A. Mathews, who was Choctaw. Counting down four generations, this would have made my father one-sixteenth Choctaw.

---

24   Glaser, *Hufstedler Family and Allied Families, p. 339*

Growing up, Ann Maria played with President Andrew Jackson's adopted children. Their back yards joined. She and her husband Abisha Curl named a son after him, Andrew Jackson Curl.

Abisha and Ann Maria were married July 21, 1836 and they had children as follows:

William 1837
Sarah Kezziah 1839
Sophronia Adeline "Fronia" 1841
Thomas 1842
John Burton 1845
Ann Maria II, December 27, 1846
Mary Jane 1850
Andrew Jackson 1852
Virginia Elizabeth "Jennie" 1855

She was made a widow when he died after being released from a Civil War Union prison camp. Three years after he died, she wrote a memory of coming to faith which has been preserved by the family. It is as follows:

July the 1st 1866
When I was about twenty-two years of age I went to a camp meeting on Cain Creek Hickman County Tenn.
I was as careless and unconcerned about the salvation of my poor soul as any one I expect. Until Monday morning the preacher talk awhile and sing and pray and while he was talking, I cannot express my feelings, nor could I get rid of them I never had such feelings before, I could not help crying and I was ashamed for anyone to see me, but I would not hide my grief, I wanted to be alone all the time, and begined to pray to the Lord to have mercy on me. I went on this way about one month, and I went to another camp meeting in Ships bend, on Saturday and after preaching mourners were called for, I refused to go up but I felt miserable and went on in this way until Sunday night, I only seemed to get worse and worse, I thought everyone was pointing the finger of scorn at me, I thought I felt more like a criminal led up to the gallows to be hung than anything else, I thought every person knew how mean I was, every one seemed to enjoy themselves but me, after they took the sacrament, mourners

were called and I became willing to go among the first, I don't know how long I was there before the Lord showed himself to me, I viewed the Father and the son sitting on his right side on the throne and all was well with me then it was the lovliest sight that I ever saw I did not feel like I could see any more trouble, but alas my days are full of trouble, next morning the doors were opened for the reception of members, and I felt it my duty to join the Methodist church, I lived with them until after I married and moved on Piny. There were several Baptists over there and it was a long time that I was neither Methodist nor Baptist nor nothing else that was any account. But at last I became attached to the old Baptist on Sunday in March 1860.

Following is another letter written by Ann Maria Curl:

I went to Union church and heard brother John A. Edwards preach a powerful sermon, from that time I had a great desire to become a member of that church, I wanted to talk with some of the brethren about but could not meet with a good opportunity, sometimes I would say something to Mr. Curl about it but he would not talk about it, so I was in trouble, I could not sleep much, I knew the Baptist did not believe in camp meetings and I thought they would not receive me, but I could not conveniently stay away so on the Saturday before the 3rd Sunday in August 1860 I ventured to talk to the church and was received and was baptized on Sunday by elder John A. Edwards.
/s/ Ann M. Curl
I have written this thinking that my children and friends could look at it when I am gone from this world.
So fare you well A.M.C.
This July the 7th 1867

As a widow she moved to Ripley County, Missouri with her daughter and son-in-law, Ann Maria II and John Wesley Hufstedler. She died at the age of eighty-two in Ripley County on August 8, 1894.

ANN MARIA CURL II:

Her name is pronounced Ann Mariah. This lady was the second wife of John Wesley Hufstedler and they were my great grandparents. They were married on September 21, 1872 and their three oldest children were born in Tennessee:

Cora 1873
John Thomas 1875
Ida, Oct 22, 1877

About 1880 they moved to Ripley County, Missouri, in a wagon train led by John Wesley's brother-in-law, Andrew J. Whitwell. The migration was made with other families who were their relatives and friends. Four more children were born in Ripley County:

Samuel Rufus 1881
Elizabeth Ann 1885
Frances "Frankie" 1887
George Washington 1889

She was a member of the Buffalo River Baptist Association of Tennessee and, after the big move to Missouri, a charter member of the Primitive Baptist Church in Ripley County. She was a midwife of some renown and often rode out side-saddle to deliver babies in the neighborhood. She delivered such family members as Horace Hufstedler, Nace Randel and Anna Randel.

THE LEWIS FAMILY

WITH RELATED FAMILIES BAKER, COMER, HALE, FORREST, McCLAREN, PEAKE

THOMAS LEWIS III AND DESCENDANTS:

Original research in Delaware and Virginia[25] offers evidence that there were three generations of men named Thomas Lewis. For clarity, I have called them Thomas I, Thomas II and Thomas III. Our proven ancestor was Thomas Lewis III. We have his Will.

Thomas Lewis I was from Delaware and Difficult Run, Loudon County, Virginia. He would have been born in the late 17th century.

Thomas Lewis II was a native of Virginia. He was a tenant farmer for Henry Fitzhugh in Fairfax County, Virginia where he raised ten children, the eldest being our Thomas III. In 1760 he was farming 100 acres for Henry Fitzhugh but owned the land where he was living, having inherited it from his father in Loudon County, Virginia on September 13, 1749. Executors for Thomas I's Will were Stephen Lewis (his brother) and Thomas Lewis, a nephew. Witnesses were John Hunter, Charles Mason and John Peake.

Thomas II died on July 15, 1771 in Fairfax County, VA. In his Will he names his wife Elizabeth and his children (not in birth order):

> **Thomas**
> James
> William
> Henry
> John
> Ann
> Sarah

---

[25] By cousin Grady Lewis

147

Jane
Frances
Winnifred

Executors of his Will were: Sarah, Thomas, James and Winnifred Lewis. Witnesses: Elijah Williams, John Barrett and Sam Weaden. Recorded 17 Sept, 1771.

In the recent past, much research has been done on our Thomas Lewis, with emphasis on his possible relationship to Fielding Lewis, husband of George Washington's sister Betty. Indeed, he named one of his own sons Fielding. DNA research has recently proven that our Thomas was not related to Fielding Lewis, the Revolutionary War patriot.

THOMAS LEWIS III:

Thomas was a Virginian, born around 1735. He grew up in Fairfax County, VA. His exact birth date is unknown to us, but he was "of age" when he witnessed a Will in 1764 and he was married around 1761. He had a very good friend named John Rhodes. Both men served in the Revolutionary War.

He was listed as a witness in a Will of Thomas Hooud of Amelia County in the Province of Virginia. Will Book 2, Page 77 dated 7 April, 1764. William Lewis, Henry Lewis, John Lewis and Francis Lewis were also recorded in this Will which was probated on 27 Sept, 1764.

Thomas Lewis III married Jane Comer Peake, the daughter of Robert Peake and Elizabeth Comer about 1761. Elizabeth Comer was the daughter of John Comer of Prince William County, Virginia.

The Lewis and Peake families moved south to Orange County, North Carolina after the Revolutionary War, most probably because of land grants to the young men in payment for their service in the Continental Army. Recently discovered documents in the North Carolina State Archives confirm two primary land grants to Thomas: The first was 165 acres on both sides of Enoe River on October 2, 1761. On December 4, 1778 he was granted 100 acres along Elliby's Creek, to-wit: Lots 1701, 1781 and 1761. Duke University now stands on some of his land.

Thomas Lewis III and Jane Comer Peake had a family of eight children. Thomas died in North Carolina in 1805 and was buried in Farthington-Lewis Cemetery in Durham, North Carolina. One of their daughters married into the Duke family of Duke University and tobacco-growing fame. Thomas left a Will and it lists extensive real and personal property as well as slaves. I have a copy of this Will in my family history records.

The children of Thomas Lewis and Jane Comer Peake were:

> Elizabeth
> Fielding
> Frances
> William
> Henry
> **John Comer I**
> Mary (Polly)
> Robert

JOHN COMER LEWIS I:

Thomas's son, **John Comer Lewis I** is our direct ancestor. He was born in 1779 near what is now Durham, North Carolina. He had three marriages in his lifetime, to-wit: Nancy Forrest (daughter of Shadrack and Jane Forrest), Elizabeth "Annie" McClaren, born in 1781, and thirdly to Agness Powell. Children were born of the first two marriages.

Children of John Comer Lewis I and Nancy Forrest:

> Thomas W. "Bill" 1798
> Henry, 1804
> Fielding, 1806
> Shadrack, 1807
> Jane, 1810

Nancy Forrest died when their daughter Jane was born. Nancy herself had come from an illustrious family. Her cousin, Nathan Bedford Forrest, was a General in the Civil War and had the dubious distinction of being instrumental in the formation of the Klu Klux Klan subsequent to that war. He was a famous Cavalry General and the maneuvers he instigated are still studied in military history.

Their grandson Shadrack met a violent end at the close of the Civil War when he was murdered by bushwhackers.

Among other things, **John Comer I** was a Baptist minister, listed in a Marriage Book in Durham, North Carolina Library. Since he was not the oldest son and did not inherit land from his father, he migrated to Middle Tennessee, traveling by oxcart and arriving soon after the removal of the Indians between 1814 and 1816, bringing his youngest children with him. He was listed as a Magistrate in Hickman County, Tennessee in 1826, the year our forefather, **John Comer II** was born. In Tennessee, **John Comer Lewis I** and his wife lived near Farmer's Exchange, about twenty miles below Centerville. He was listed as co-founder of Goshen Baptist Church and owned land on Cane Creek where his sons Shadrack and Fielding built the first carding mill for processing wool fibers in 1830.[26]

He and his second wife, Elizabeth "Annie" McClaren were married in 1816 and had the following children:

> Sarah, born 1818
> Daniel M., 1820
> Susan, born 821
> Nancy, born 1822
> Elizabeth "Betty",1823
> Thomas William, 1824
> **John Comer II, April 18, 1824**
> Samuel, 1831

Wife Annie McClaren died in 1831 and he was married a third time to Agness Powell on April 29, 1834. There were no children of this marriage.

JOHN COMER LEWIS II, The Soldier:

Our ancestor **John Comer Lewis II** lived a busy and productive life, though a fairly short one by our standards. He died of injuries sustained in the Civil War, most probably gunshot left in his body which caused him illness and death at fifty-two, some fifteen years after he was injured at the Battle of Shiloh. When he was twenty, he joined

---

26   Spence's History of Hickman County, Tennessee

the Hickman Guards, primarily formed to protect property and families from unfriendly Indians still marauding the area. But a contingent of the Guards also fought in the Mexican War. With others, **John Comer II** was sent to Mexico and fought in the battle of Monterrey, Mexico on September 24, 1846. He was listed as a member of a Bible class organized among the Hickman Guards while they were in Mexico. Almost worse than the battle they fought was dysentery experienced by practically all of them because of polluted water.[27]

Upon his return to Hickman County he married Ruth Lloyd Baker about 1848, daughter of Dr. Thomas R. Baker and Ruth Rhodica Lloyd. Some years after their marriage they moved to Howell County, Missouri and Fulton County, Arkansas with Ruth's parents and two of her brothers, along with their families. John Comer bought farmland there around 1861. Fulton and Howell Counties bordered the Missouri-Arkansas state line and at least one of his properties was partly in Missouri and partly in Arkansas. His Howell County, Missouri property was purchased November 3, 1860. He owned three farms according to his son, James Hale Lewis.[28] He and his family appear on the 1860 Howell County, Missouri Federal Census.

He enlisted in the Confederate States Army on July 26, 1861 at Camp Shaver, Arkansas; he was 35 years old and left his wife Ruth at home with five children. He served as a Private in Company I, 7th Regiment, Arkansas Infantry under Captain Milton D. Barber. He was wounded, but reported dead, at the Battle of Shiloh on Sunday, April 6, 1862. "An ounce of lead struck him in the right side. The bullet was cut out at his back."[29] His wife, Ruth Baker, remained at their farm with the children after his reported death.

The children of John Comer Lewis II and Ruth Baker:

> Rhodesia "Docia", Nov 28, 1849
> Louisa Elizabeth "Bettie", Jan 5, 1853
> Nancy Caroline, Aug 14, 1855
> John Comer III, Mar 14, 1857
> **James Hale,** Dec 4, 1860

---

[27] Spence's History. ibid
[28] From a letter written by James Hale Lewis, John Comer's son, to Ezra Lewis, a nephew on February 2, 1933, in my files.
[29] Ibid.

One night in the fall of 1862 there was a call at the gate: "Is this where the widow Lewis lives?" The youngest child, James Hale, recalled that his sister Docia sat straight up in her bed and exclaimed: "That's Pap!"[30] The family all arose to have such a memorable family reunion that Jim vividly remembered it until his dying day and could never retell it without tears. He was less than three years old at the time.

After his injury, "Pap" had first been cared for by a farm couple near the battle site and later hospitalized at Chattanooga, Tennessee. He was granted a disability discharge October 13, 1862 and, after recovering from his wounds, walked home from the hospital where he received treatment, about 375 miles as the crow flies. He would have had a hard trip; besides his weakness from the injury he would have had to avoid soldiers and mercenaries who roamed the hills and valleys looking for deserters.

Sadly, John Comer's wife, Ruth Baker, died of unknown causes to us, just three months after his return in early 1863. John Comer struggled on in Arkansas for another eighteen months but the grieving widower with his little children finally returned to his roots in Hickman County, Tennessee in September, 1864. His oldest child was fifteen and youngest not yet four years old. He sold at least one of his farms for Confederate money to his brother-in-law, Noahdiah Baker. This money was worthless, of course, after the war ended. In Tennessee, he hired Martha Jane Thornton to help him with the family and eventually married her. They had five more children:

> William Whitney, 1869
> Samuel M., 1870
> Molly, 1872
> George W., 1873
> Ruth

Once again the family was on the move; they joined other families migrating back west by covered wagon to Missouri. He first purchased a home in West Plains in 1870, just north of his Arkansas property. In 1876 John Comer purchased a farm in northwestern Ripley County, Missouri in the community of Big Barren where I lived as a child and a year later

---

[30]   Ibid.

sold the home in West Plains, Missouri on November 6, 1877. John Comer II made his Will in June, 1878 and died in Ripley County November 3, 1878. He was buried in the Old Lewis Cemetery, located on the southern portion of that farm, and just south of the Cave Spring Branch.

He lived quite a full and adventurous life, having served in two wars and migrating from Tennessee to Arkansas and Missouri, back to Tennessee and finally to Southern Missouri. He was only fifty-two at the time of his death. I asked Aunt Zelma if she knew why he died so young. As if I should have known, she replied, "He died of complications of his war injuries, of course."

In his Will he separated the farm to bequeath half to each of his two separate families, to-wit: The first family by Ruth Baker was willed the northern portion of the farm, including the Lewis Cave, and the southern portion was bequeathed to his wife Martha J. Thornton and her children. Much of the northern portion of the farm was still wilderness and had not been cleared for crops.

JAMES HALE LEWIS, The Scholar:

James Hale and Abbie May Lewis

My maternal grandfather, James Hale Lewis, loved learning almost above all else, reading everything he could lay his hands on, including the encyclopedia, his children's high school text books, and the Holy Bible. He was born in Northern Arkansas just before the Civil War broke out but thereafter lived most of his younger years in Tennessee with his older siblings, his father, his step-mother and half-brothers and sisters. As often happens, there was domestic unrest in this combined family. His step-mother favored her own children and he often felt unloved. As a teenager the family returned to Missouri. His father was suffering from Civil War injuries so much of the heavier work of this rural family went to Jim. When he reached young adulthood he was able to attend a teachers' institute at Fairdealing, Missouri to fulfill his ambition to teach and in his mid-twenties, taught Little Barren School where he met his future wife, one of his young students, Abbie May Glore, who was ten years younger than he.

On December 26, 1886 **James Hale Lewis** married **Abbie May Glore**, not quite sixteen years old. Abbie was a strong-willed young lady and, upon her first glimpse of James Hale, who was riding down the road on his horse, said to her then-companion: "I'm going to marry that man (if I never get him!)" Later, when James Hale went to her parents to get permission to marry Abbie, she informed her parents that if they didn't let her marry him, she would run away with him. So her parents finally gave reluctant permission and they were married before preacher Morgan Cotton at the Glore home on Buffalo Creek, Ripley County, Missouri. Abbie's little brother, Samuel Ernest, had little regard for his brother-in-law Jim and perhaps it was because of the wide difference in their ages.

As a married couple, Jim and Abbie were looked up to in the community, sought after for assistance in home births, deaths, accidents, as well as happy occasions. They both nursed many folks in and around Big Barren during the flu epidemic of 1917-19 and never contracted the virus themselves. Granddad read widely and had a layman's knowledge of medicine, practiced hygiene and followed the latest medical discoveries.

Jim eventually purchased his siblings' portions of the Lewis farm and became sole owner of the northern portion of the farm. One Indenture has been found, dated March 22, 1889, between John C. and Isabel Bell-Lewis and James H. Lewis recording the sale of one-eighth interest of this farm to James H. Lewis for $70.00. The north portion of the farm consisted of some cleared farmland and some native scrub brush and timber on flatland and hilly wooded areas. The land was never rich, but was rocky and subject to spring flooding which carried off much of the good soil. Jim, however, was a scholar, mainly self-taught, and practiced crop rotation on his farmland. His daughter Zelma Lewis-Henderson remembers his anger at neighboring farmers who refused to believe in crop rotation and planted corn year after year, depleting the soil on other farms in the community.

A dispute arose between the two Lewis families as to which family owned one certain field near the Cave Spring Branch. It was taken to court to resolve and, despite the fact that the Will stated the farm should be divided by the Cave Spring Branch and all fields north of the Branch would belong to the "first family" Lewises, the Judge ruled just the opposite and granted it to the "second family" Lewises. It might be interesting to note that the sitting Judge in the matter was none other than Samuel Ernest "Ernest" Glore, Jim's brother-in-law, and they never particularly liked each other! Ernest was a life-long Republican and Jim was a staunch Democrat.

Jim continued to teach school in the county for twenty years. It was his true profession because he had such an abiding love and passion for learning. Jim and Abbie lived in various places for awhile, finding a home in the vicinity of whatever school Jim was teaching. Their first born child, little William Albert, was born while they lived in the Pine Community. He only lived for seven months and was buried in the Pine Cemetery. Eventually Jim gave up teaching and they settled on the Lewis farm, first living in a small cabin adjacent to a well in one of the fields. They then built a log house on top of a small hill just north of Lewis Cave. Jim believed it was healthier up there and, besides, the spring floods would not invade their place. Of course the family had to carry water up the hill from the well in the field for all the years they lived there, but by that time there were enough children to share the task. They eventually dug a cistern at the log house on the hill to catch winter water run-off, but this cistern would always go dry in the summertime. The younger daughters were born in the log house on top of the hill and lived there until time to attend high school in Doniphan.

The children of James Hale Lewis and Abbie May Glore were:

William Albert, Jan 8, 1888
John Comer, July 6, 1889
Samuel Augustus, Aug 17, 1891
Robert Edward Lee, July 24, 1893
James Herschel, June 11, 1895
Chester Earl, Oct 10, 1896
Ruth Jane, Dec 12, 1899
Virgil Jackson, Mar 16, 1903
Velda Theresa, Aug 18, 1905
Edna Mae, Mar 2, 1907
Elsie Beatrice, Mar 28, 1909
Violet Zelma, July 1, 1914

In a day and age when many children died in childhood from disease, only one of Jim and Abbie Lewis's children died in infancy. James Hale is credited with saving the lives of the other eleven children. His ambitious reading on any subject available made him somewhat of a layman's doctor. When the little ones would get diarrhea, which was called summer complaint and was attributed to many things such as feeding the baby mashed green peas, but was actually caused by fly infestation during the summer months, James Hale would forbid Abbie to nurse them, but would actually on occasion carry the baby in his arms and let it cry, not allowing its mother to feed it. He would then scrape green apples and feed the baby; enough to prevent dehydration and massive loss of minerals. Nowadays mothers feed sick babies a commercial liquid formula of minerals with many of the same minerals as green apple. The young sisters were sometimes fed mare's milk after an illness, which was believed to have healing and extra-nutritious properties.

Until his dying day Jim Lewis read to improve his mind. One incident illustrates his wide-spread reading. To supplement his income, son-in-law and my father, Elmer Randel, who lived down the road, often hauled loads to market with his stake-bed truck. Loads included such diverse things as railroad ties, farm produce or whatever was available. He left home one day with a load on the truck and, when nightfall came, did not return. There were no telephones in the community so the family was unaware what happened to him until the next day when the mailman brought word from Doniphan, from Aunt Zelma Lewis-Henderson, that Elmer had taken seriously ill with pneumonia and was in bed at her house under the doctor's care. James Hale had recently read of a new "miracle drug" (Sulfa—the first antibiotic) and had the mailman take a note to Doniphan to have the doctor send right away to St. Louis and get this miracle drug. But the doctor was one step ahead of Granddad and had already been administering Sulfa around the clock and by midnight on the first night he received it, Elmer's fever was breaking. For sure he would have died without it. The point, however, is that Jim Lewis was so well-read he wanted to instruct the doctor on the latest remedy!

In a letter to a niece written in the early 1930's, James Hale testified to the fact that his parents were members of the Primitive Baptist Church. He indicated that it was not too popular a branch of the Baptists at that time. He went on to affirm a tenet of the Primitive Baptists; strict Calvinism—that is, God has placed each name of his chosen ones in his Book of Life, and there is no deviation from that!

James Hale Lewis lived to be eighty-two years old, dying on February 15, 1943. He suffered from undiagnosed palsy the last ten years or so of his life and would become quite out of patience when he could hardly get his coffee cup to his mouth without spilling its contents. But he remained in good spirits, always sitting in his chair, reading to improve his mind and studying the Bible.

He was a storehouse of wisdom for those around him and esteemed by family and neighbors alike. His son-in-law Elmer Randel looked up to him as a father figure and always called him Dad Jim, which name was accepted and subsequently used by Jim's own children.

He died quietly of heart failure one early morning as he sat in his chair, putting on his shoes.

EDNA MAE LEWIS RANDEL:

My mother, Edna Mae Lewis, third from the youngest of a family of twelve whose parents were James Hale Lewis and Abbie May Glore was married to my father, Elmer Folk Randel, in 1929.

When Mom was a child at home, she felt herself inferior to her older sister Velda. Mom had some scars on her head caused from boils and her thin hair didn't quite cover these scars. All her life she lamented that when visitors would come, they would look at sister Velda and say, "My, what a beautiful child." They would then just look at my mother and not say anything. She took this to mean that she was an ugly child. She, in turn, in the inevitable pecking order of families, brow-beat her next youngest sister Elsie. She was, however, treasured by some of her older brothers who would carry her around on their shoulders. And she loved the orange found annually in the toe of her stocking on Christmas morning.

She carried childhood fears into adulthood. She was particularly fearful of closed-in places and, especially small spaces under houses. Her parents and older siblings would scare the youngsters with stories that "old rawhide and bloody bones" would get them if they went under the house. Of course this was to prevent their getting bitten by any stray snakes under the house, but it did not help Mom and her siblings when it came to phobias.

When Edna reached an age to attend high school, she left the log home of her parents in the Big Barren community of Ripley County and went to Doniphan, the County Seat, to attend high school. She stayed with her older brother and his wife, Samuel Augustus Lewis and Bertha Shaw-Lewis. I have never heard this, but I feel sure that her parents paid "board" to them, perhaps in the form of produce, milk and eggs.

Mom attended two years of high school in Doniphan and thereafter taught school after passing the Missouri State teacher's examination. She taught at Upper Barren School and Running Water School, riding her horse, Old Snappy, from home. She recalls getting on Old Snappy for the ride home from school and being too tired to guide the horse. He knew the way home anyway, and she would just drop the reins, give him a gentle kick in the flanks, and let him go. I met a little old man in October, 1997 who recalled that my Mother had taught him how to speak English back in the 1920s when he entered school. He was a little boy of German emigrant parents and his name was Eddie Forister.

But while still living in Doniphan she met her true love, Elmer Folk Randel. She was in a group of teenagers who would go for rides on a Sunday afternoon. Elmer's cousin Horace Hufstedler had an automobile, or had the use of his father's vehicle, and would take several for Sunday drives. He wanted Mom to be his "date" but she said she always hoped that Elmer would ask her first. Then, on one happy occasion, Elmer said: "When we go on Sunday drives, I would like it understood that you will always be with me." Music to my mother's ears.

After teaching for two years Mom went to St. Louis to work, following Elmer who already had a job at Chevrolet Motors. It was there that she and Dad eloped to St. Charles, MO. Mom was living with Aunt Ada Ertle at the time, Grandma Lewis's older sister. She recalled to me: "On the Saturday morning we were going to elope, I put on my 'wedding' dress and watched for him at the front window. When I saw him coming, all dressed up in suit and tie, I thought he was the handsomest man I had ever seen."

Upon their return from the marriage ceremony, they told Aunt Ada their news and she refused to believe them. She sent her son back across the Missouri River to St. Charles to see the Justice of the Peace for confirmation. For years afterwards Mom worried about being legally married since, even though they had a proper marriage license, there were no witnesses to the ceremony except the Justice and his wife.

My brother Wilton Lewis and I were born in St. Louis. When I was still an infant our family returned to Ripley County. The Great Depression was in full swing and there was hardly any work in St. Louis. Dad had held his job at the Chevrolet plant longer than most because he was in charge of keeping large batteries viable even when the plant was closed. Granddad and Grandma Lewis deeded my parents a parcel on their farm upon which Dad built a house. The property was in a field facing the Lewis Cave. Dad and Mom were a couple who had a good marriage, worked hard and raised us children to be upstanding citizens. I do not remember hearing them quarrel or say unkind things to one another. It was understood that Dad was the final authority in the family. Mom sometimes made an "end run" behind Dad's back to accomplish certain things she thought were important, mostly seeing that we children had advantages that Dad was not willing to fund.

Dad also electrified the Lewis Cave and made a footpath about one-fourth mile through to the end of the easily accessible portion of the cave. He and Mom erected signs and advertised for tourists and Mom was often the tour guide. Limited numbers came, but the rural roads prevented any tourist boom.

Mom worked very hard during those depression years. She planted a large garden every year and worked like a slave in the hot summer kitchen to can enough vegetables and fruit to feed us through the winter. She organized and taught a Sunday School class at the Big Barren Baptist Church and entertained and fed dozens of city cousins who came to the country in the summertime on holiday.

During the early 1940's Mom completed her high school work by correspondence course and received a completion certificate. She taught Big Barren Elementary School the year I was in the seventh grade, 1943-44.

We left Ripley County during World War II chiefly because my brother Wilton Lewis Randel was ready for high school and Mom and Dad did not want him living away from home to continue his education. We moved to Detroit, Michigan where Aunt Ruth, Mom's oldest sister, and Uncle John Bell lived. They enticed our family with promises of lots of work in the defense plants.

Mom and Dad both worked during those latter war years, often six and seven days a week, in defense plants. Mom worked in the Briggs Factory. After the war was over Mom worked for the State of Michigan Unemployment Association. My father's health deteriorated and doctors recommended moving to a hot, dry climate. So in the fall of 1947, after selling our home and furnishings, Dad purchased a brand new car, a brand new house trailer and we headed west.

It was hard on Wilton and me; Wilton was a senior and I was a junior in high school. We parked in Tucson, Arizona at 614 Delano Avenue where we finished out the school year at Amphitheatre High School, with Willie graduating, but it became so very hot in that little house trailer that Dad hitched it up and we continued west, eventually settling in Riverside, California in the summer of 1948 at Highgrove Court, 220 La Cadena Drive. I remember Mom that winter in Tucson, cleaning and cooking in that little home on wheels. Dust storms often swirled through the trailer, leaving grit and sand on newly cleaned floors and counters. She sewed a western costume for me to wear to school—denim skirt and plaid blouse.

After moving to Riverside, Mom soon found employment with Burpee Seed Company at first, then the Federal Farm Subsidy program and, finally, at Security Title Insurance Company where she eventually became head bookkeeper and an officer in the company. She retired at 61 after which she and Dad toured all 50 states of the United States, all of the contiguous states and Alaska by camper. They also saw much of Canada and flew to American Samoa during the time my sister Emily and Ron Needham and family lived there.

My mother, a descendant of Revolutionary War soldier Thomas Lewis of Durham, North Carolina, died in Riverside, California in June of 2005 at the age of 98 years and 98 days.

THE GLORE FAMILY
WITH RELATED FAMILIES JACKSON AND HORINE

Johann Michael Klor, German immigrant of the Glore family, a miner by trade, came to the New World with his wife and family in 1717. He was the son of Hans Martin Klaar and his wife Maria Barbara and was born about 1687. In the late twentieth century, the names of Johann Michael Klor and his family were found in an ancient record book in a Lutheran church in Alsace Lorraine, with the following entry:

> "12 July 1717, the following listed parents, together with their children, expect to move away from here, wanting to take ship to PA, and there in the hardship of the wilderness better their piece of bread than they could here...."

The name Klor appears in several forms. In the birth register of the old Hebron Lutheran Church near Madison Court House, Virginia, which is written in German and begins with the year 1750, the name appears as Klor. Other spellings are found in civil records such as Clawr, Klaar, Clore, Glore.[31] Our branch of the family has been spelled Glore ever since they moved to Kentucky in 1795.

At the time of their immigration, Johann Michael Klor's family was made up of his wife, Anna Barbara and their children:

Agness Margaretha 1711
Andreas Claus   1713
Johann George   1716

Other children, Maria Barbara and Hans Michael, died in Germany as young children. They had at least two more children after they arrived in Virginia:

Catherine 1715
Margaret 1719

---

[31] The Clore-Glore Family by Dr. Arthur Leslie Keith, 1938.

1726
Johannes aft 1717

They headed to England for passage with the larger group, all miners, who were making this life-changing move. Upon arrival in London they discovered that their ship's Captain Tarbett of the ship *Scott,* with whom they had contracted to make the crossing to Pennsylvania, was in debtor's prison. There was no choice, they had to wait it out until the Captain was released, by which time their meager savings had been exhausted and they had no money for passage. After Captain Tarbett's release, they approached him and asked for passage to Pennsylvania anyway, promising that they would repay him when they earned the passage money after arrival in the New World. He agreed. It was an arduous voyage and many died from disease and malnutrition.

It is unclear why the ship did not land in Pennsylvania but, instead, landed in Virginia where Captain Tarbett refused to release them until they paid for their passage. Acting Governor Alexander Spotswood of Virginia, a prosperous landowner, paid the Captain for their passage and, in return, the passengers signed an agreement to become his indentured servants for seven years. Governor Spotswood was convinced that his property in the mountains west of Tidewater Virginia held treasures of gold and he was determined to discover it. He never did.

Seven years to work as a veritable slave in Spotswood's mine! But they had no choice. Spotswood settled them in a community along with an earlier wave of miners from the Old World called, appropriately, Germanna, located about twenty miles from Fredericksburg. After a disagreement on the length of their indenture, the matter was finally settled and in 1724 or 1725 and they removed in a body about thirty miles due west to the Robinson River Valley in present Madison County. Petitioning the Governor and the House of Burgesses, they asked for redress of their grievances, which was so granted. They then had license to collect money, build a church and call a minister. In a few years they were able to send Michael and two others back to Germany to bring a Lutheran minister for their company of believers. Their Hebron Lutheran Church building was built in 1740 and still holds regular services

Hebron Lutheran Church today

Johann Michael Klor was an industrious man and he began acquiring land soon after his indenture was completed. At the time of his death he was well-to-do, owning more than a square mile of land. His will reveals much property, including seven slaves, and numerous notes and bonds, some in large amounts. It appears that he was able to fulfill to some degree the role of a banker.[32] He and his extended family lived in the area for the next two or three generations and then branched out, some moving south and others moving west, always looking for available land. However, to this day, there are Clores living in Madison County and a Clore Furniture Factory is still in business there. Our grandson Jackson Hale Wilder has a child's walnut rocker purchased by Dick and me when we visited the factory in 1997.

In 1795 great grandson Samuel Glore and his family moved west to Oldham County, Kentucky where the men continued as miners in the coal mines. Samuel and his wife Frances Christopher are our direct ancestors. Their children:

> Harriet
> Allen C.
> Matilda
> Eliza

[32]   The Clore-Glore Family, p 12.

Elizabeth
Norbin Samuel
Morton Christopher
Milburn
Lisbon Alexander 1812

The west, however, continued to fascinate, probably for the possibility of acquiring more land in the ever-expanding new country. So the family once again moved west, this time settling in Washington County, Missouri, just south of St. Louis, where the families acquired property and the men worked the lead and tiff[33] mines. Towns in the area named *Rich Woods, Old Miles,* and *Bonne Terre,* are all indicative of mining in that county. Another interesting community name is "Germanna" which, of course, harkens back to the town in Virginia first occupied by our Klor ancestor. My grandmother, Abbie May Glore, went to school in Germanna, Missouri. She never spoke of learning any German so perhaps the school was conducted in English.

LISBON ALEXANDER GLORE:

Lisbon was one of the emigrants from Kentucky to Missouri, according to his grandson Samuel Ernest Glore. He would have been a young married man of twenty-four, because records show that they moved in 1836-37. He married Katherine Wells May 16, 1833 and their first child was born before their big move to Missouri.[34]

Settling in Missouri, they owned a spacious farm in Washington County and he is buried in a small cemetery on this farm.[35] There is no marker. In September of 2000 Dick and I went to Washington County looking for some of my history. The Missouri Highway Department directed us to a primitive cemetery in a farmer's field which would have been Lisbon's farm. The farm is still fertile and rich looking, some 160 years later. Children of Lisbon Glore and Katherine Wells:

---

[33] Tiff is a by-product of lead.
[34] Census Records.
[35] Traveling west on Route 47, turn left at Providence Baptist Church onto Ter de Lac. Then turn right on St. Francois Road. The cemetery is 5.3 miles along, on a bank over the right-hand side of the road. There is no direction marker on the road to the cemetery.

Mary Frances 1836
William Morton "Will" 1837
Emily Ann 1840
Sarah E. 1842
Eliza Jane 1844
Martha L. 1846
John Milburn 1848
Isabelle "Belle" 1851
Lisbon Alexander II "Bub" 1858

WILLIAM MORTON GLORE:

Born on August 26, 1837, William Morton Glore lived his whole life in Missouri. He was born in Washington County, in Ebo, near Potosi. The community of Ebo is only a memory except in local history books, but there remains a little rural church called, *Soule's Chapel*, where Will probably worshiped as a child and where some of our family members are buried in the adjacent cemetery.

William Morton was drafted into the Union Army in the latter part of the Civil War. He was enrolled at Ironton, Washington County, Missouri on September 20, 1864, listing his occupation as "miner." He served in the Army as a Private with Company H of the 15th Missouri Infantry and was mustered out at Nashville, Tennessee nine months later on June 16, 1865. According to his son Ernest, he was never in a battle but drew a pension after the war just the same. The vital statistics in his military records reveal that William Morton was a small man, 5 feet 2½ inches tall, black hair, grey eyes and dark complexion. He was mild-mannered, quiet, but was known to possess a wonderful sense of humor.

He and Nancy Jane Jackson were already married when he was drafted into the Army and his little daughter Emily Frances was about a year old. They were married in Old Mines, Washington County on November 8, 1862, one of the first marriages of record in that County. Their children:

Emily Frances 1863
Ada Cora 1866
Susan Catherine "Suzie" 1868
Twins   **(Abbie May, February 12, 1871**

(Albert Preston, February 12, 1871
Samuel Ernest, 1874

It is not known if Will went back to mining after his discharge or if he worked the land, but after another nineteen years, early in the year 1884, Will and Nancy started looking around for another place to settle. He had a healthy family, mostly teenagers, but able-bodied and available to work the land. William Morton's sister, Mary Frances Glore, had married a man named Williamson "Bill" Gibson and this couple had moved to Ripley County in Southern Missouri. They wrote Will, painting a rosy picture of the climate in Ripley County, asserting that one's livestock could feed off the land in the wintertime because of the supposed mildness of the climate. Will and Nancy decided to move.

An account of the journey came from ten year old Ernest:

> We departed to the south from Washington County, taking a covered wagon with a team of horses and a cow tied on behind the wagon. Traveling with us in another covered wagon was my oldest sister, Emily Frances, her husband Tom House and their little son Ernest, who was named after me. The journey took five days and nights. I well remember the trip even though I was a young boy of only ten years. We heard wolves howling in the thick, dark woods at night. I was very frightened, sleeping in that flimsy wagon. The first night we camped at the north prong of the Little Black River where the horses got into quicksand and our whole family had to labor to free them. The last night on the road was spent in a camp at Van Buren on the Current River. There was no bridge across the Current so we had to cross by ferry, tying the cow behind the wagon. She was mooing and digging her feet into the dirt but we managed to drag her onto the ferry. After the river crossing, we traveled over a ridge into Little Barren and there met a man tracking a bear. "Sleep in my house tonight," the hunter urged. "You won't have to bed down in the woods and be in danger of attack." Needless to say, we were very happy to accept his hospitality in the safety of his cabin.

The family settled on some land bordered by Little Barren Creek that brother-in-law Williamson "Bill" Gibson, a minister, sold them. They had arrived early enough in summer to plant corn and were able to harvest it before they learned that there was a problem with the ownership of the land they bought from Gibson. They had to relocate. After harvest that summer, Will took his corn over to the Eleven Point River to a mill to get it ground into cornmeal. Eleven Point River runs in the western part of the county and is some distance from Little Barren Creek, several hours of travel with horse-drawn wagon.

Ernest recalls living in a rough lumber cabin in "abject poverty." They often had nothing to eat but molasses and cornbread. The daughters "fried" the molasses to make them thicker and easier to spread on their cornbread, but mother Nancy Jane, fearful that the supply of molasses would be exhausted, finally made them stop because the molasses cooked down to a thicker consistency and was eaten in larger quantities. Ernest related that he loved to go over to Uncle Bill and Aunt Mary Gibson's because they had biscuits for breakfast; quite a treat for him.

After learning that their land wasn't rightfully theirs, they relocated to the Pine community that winter, moving north in Ripley County in deep snow with the horses and cow laboring through the drifts and the family huddling, once again, in the covered wagon. Will subsequently had a falling out with Pete Camp, the landlord of the land they rented at Pine over a division of crops, and eventually moved back south, still in Ripley County, and settled on the south prong of Buffalo Creek in a house with a wooden chimney. Little Ernest recalled many fires in the wooden chimney that would have to be extinguished to prevent the house from burning down.

The younger children attended school at Little Barren and Abbie May fell in love with the teacher, James Hale Lewis, a handsome young man ten years older than she. The feeling was mutual, and after some time passed, Jim came to call on the elder Glores to ask for Abbie's hand in marriage. Ernest, the family storyteller, related in later years his version of the meeting:

"When schoolteacher Jim Lewis came to our home to reveal his intention to marry Abbie, rather than asking for father's permission, he said: 'Mr. Glore, I am going to marry your daughter Abbie. What are you going to do about it?' Abbie was not quite sixteen years old and Jim was twenty-five. I never liked that man after that encounter," related Ernest.

Ernest was the last living person to tell this story so it has never been authenticated. On the other hand, the Lewis family told the story with a different twist:

Abbie said, "When Jim came to the house, I told my mother and father that I was going to marry that man and if they didn't let me, I would run away with him."

Whichever way the encounter happened between parents, suitor and daughter, the fact remains that she was very young to be married but subsequently spent sixty years as his wife. They were married on December 26, 1886 at the family home.

~ ~ ~ ~

Will had a tragic logging accident four years later on August 2, 1890 while living on Buffalo Creek. He lost his left leg below the knee. An article in the *Prospect News* records the tragic accident:

"Last Friday morning while William Glore, living on Buffalo, was engaged in hauling saw logs, he had the misfortune to fall from his loaded wagon. His left leg was caught under the wheels and his ankle and the bones of the foot and the smaller leg bone were horribly crushed, part of the bones protruding through the flesh. Dr. Sam Proctor of this place[36] was sent for and went up at once and, assisted by Dr. Miller of Buffalo, amputated the leg just below the fracture."

> Ernest, then sixteen years old, wrote of this at a later time in the *Prospect News*:
> "The operation was performed in the home. While the Dr. sawed the bone, Daddy Glore, under the influence of chloroform, was talking, using the same language I presume he used when he was lying on the ground with a crushed foot. After his foot was removed, Ab Ponder and I took it out and buried it in the garden."

The Glore family, while living on the south prong of Buffalo Creek, attended the Hardshell Baptist Church below Bennett. William Whitwell

---

[36]   Doniphan, Missouri, the County seat.

was the pastor of this church during those years. They moved around some in the county but never far from one place to another. After living on Little Barren Creek, Will purchased some property called the "Sink Hole Place." It had two houses on the land but only one well. Still later, they decided to move to Big Barren and sold the Sink Hole Place to their youngest son, Ernest, after the young man married beautiful Mary Eudora Horner in 1897. After their years living at Big Barren, Will and Nancy moved to Doniphan to be near Ernest, who by then was living there.

My mother, Edna Mae Lewis, one of their granddaughters, remembers her grandparents when they lived across the field from her home on Big Barren Creek. Their house was built on a hillock overlooking a spacious farmer's field belonging to Abbie and Jim Lewis and with a distant view of beautiful Ozark woods. The house was a simple wood structure with a commanding stone fireplace in the living room, one bedroom, a lean-to kitchen with cellar underneath. The cellar was entered through a trap door in the kitchen floor. There was also "the room," as they called it, off the front porch which was used as storage. As was typical in many tiny homes during that period, the living room contained a bed as part of the furnishings as well as a dining table and chairs. Outbuildings included a barn and a fine log cabin used for hay or corn storage. The house and outbuildings, though vacant, still stand today.

William Morton and Nancy Jane Glore

My mother would often cross the field to see Grandma and Grandpa Glore. By the time of her remembrance they were fairly advanced in age and Edna Mae was expected to help them out with writing letters and perhaps helping in the kitchen. Nancy Jane would dictate letters to Edna, saying "Now set this down...." So while Nancy Jane dictated and Edna Mae faithfully copied down every word, William Morton played his fiddle, sitting before the fireplace in an ancient cane-bottomed chair belonging to his father Lisbon. The chair is still in our family, owned by my brother Willie.

Another granddaughter, Zelma Lewis Henderson, Edna's youngest sister, has vivid memories of running across the field to Grandma and Grandpa Glore's house with her fingers plugging up her ears so she wouldn't hear snakes rustling in the grass. She remembers getting a special treat of one or two cookies from a tin box which had been shipped from St. Louis. Zelma related with a smile, "I would watch for a good chance to help myself to a couple more of those forbidden treats."

Zelma also remembers that Will and Nancy Jane fussed at one another more than a little bit. Nancy was a very strong-willed woman and extremely sober-minded and she would sometimes get disgusted with Will's laughter and good times. When Nancy's sister Catherine "Kit" would come to visit she enjoyed laughing and joking with Will. On one such visit when Kit and William Morton were having some fun and enjoying one another's company, Nancy Jane lost her temper and in a somewhat jealous rage remarked: "Well, why don't you two just get together and get out of here!"

Zelma remembers on more than one occasion watching Nancy Jane help peg-legged William Morton up on his horse, Old Nell. She would lift up a large old split hickory basket filled with eggs and he would ride off down the lane to take the eggs to Bennett to the nearest general store, to exchange for staple food such as sugar, coffee and flour. Under her breath, Nancy Jane would murmur, "Well, joy go with him and peace stay behind."

William Morton died in Doniphan, Missouri on January 29, 1931, at the age of 93 years and five months.

Please refer to the Jackson family for a more complete biography of Nancy Jane Jackson Glore.

ABBIE MAY GLORE LEWIS

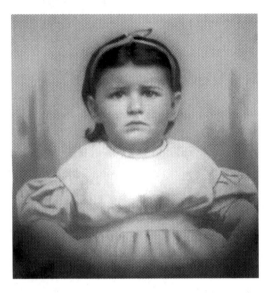

My beloved grandmother Abbie was the daughter of a Civil War soldier who fought for the Union. For almost two centuries in America, the Glores were miners, coming from Germany in 1717, settling in Virginia. Our branch of this Klor-Clore-Glore family migrated west to Kentucky and then continued west to settle in Washington County, Missouri, just south of St. Louis, before finally moving to Ripley County in 1884.

Abbie was a twin. She and her brother Albert Preston were born as fourth and fifth children to William Morton and Nancy Jane Glore. She attended elementary school at Germanna School in Washington County, Missouri and when she was about fifteen the family migrated south to Ripley County in a covered wagon.

As an adult she was tiny, just under five feet tall and always slender. When working in the garden she would wear her bonnet and a long sleeved dress to keep the sun from damaging her complexion. On the surface, Abbie was a mild-mannered person, slow to anger yet with a heart of steel. These character traits stood her in good stead, because she married very young—not quite sixteen—and became the mother of twelve children. She and husband James Hale Lewis raised eleven of these children to adulthood in a rural setting without many amenities which we would now consider necessities. She never forgot her mother's admonition that she had Jackson blood in her veins, meaning that she must maintain a strong backbone and be a leader among her peers. Jackson blood, to her mother, meant that she was related to Stonewall Jackson, hero of the Civil War. Research in recent years has proven this connection untrue.

Abbie and Jim lived in various places around the county while Jim pursued his chosen profession—teaching. They eventually settled in a north field of the John Comer Lewis farm; Jim was partial owner by inheritance of this farm. Jim quit teaching and took up farming full time, buying out his brothers and sisters until the Lewis farm totally belonged to him. They sunk a well in the field and lived in a small place until they decided to build a log house on the hill above the well. Jim felt living would be healthier for the family at the higher elevation. They sunk a cistern there, but it went dry every summer, so the family carried water from the well in the field or from the springs in the cave, which never went dry. During the years they lived in the log house on the hill, Abbie supplemented their meager livelihood by becoming the postmistress at Short, Missouri. The post office was in the living room of their log house. She made a small profit off each piece of mail that went out and was able to ship her cream and eggs to town by the post at a reduced price. Her earnings bought staples such as sugar, salt and coffee. At holiday time there was usually an orange in the toe of the children's stockings.

Abbie was the neighborhood midwife and amateur nurse, called upon to help other families in times of crisis. She and Jim went immediately to help when a neighbor died and most often in time of illness. During the deadly flu epidemic of 1918 they nursed the whole community and managed never to contract the ailment themselves.

Abbie not only fed her family of eleven by keeping a large garden and canning vegetables and fruit for the winter and preserving meat in the smoke house, but made their clothes including knitted caps, socks and gloves. She washed with a hot kettle of water in the back yard and a scrub board using home-made soap. She never had the benefit of electricity or running water in any of her homes. She quilted and ticked all their bed clothes, made mattresses from straw and feathers and cooked on an old iron stove using wood for fuel. Should unexpected company come to the house, she would head for the back yard, catch a chicken, wring its neck, scald the feathers off, clean and cut it up, take it into the kitchen to fry in a black iron skillet filled with bacon grease or home-made lard, and serve a meal which usually included mashed potatoes, green vegetables, either canned or fresh from the garden, hot biscuits or cornbread, and have it on the table in little over an hour. She lived to eighty-seven, proving that hard work never hurt anybody.

When I was a child, my beloved grandparents lived up the road from us, about a quarter mile, in their house constructed in the early 1930's. At a very young age I had permission to walk up to their house by myself to visit. I had complete run of their house and I made use of that privilege, opening dresser drawers, kitchen cupboards and especially the warming oven over the cook stove to see if any bacon was left over from breakfast. If so, I knew I was welcome to help myself. Going down the basement steps, I had permission to pick out a jar of canned food to eat for my lunch with them. There was no contest—it was always a quart mason jar of canned blackberries. My brother and I used to play in their upstairs bedroom, pulling out the Civil War era trunk from the attic area to play with the Confederate money therein and to read old love letters.

In her later years, Abbie's mother, Nancy Jane Jackson Glore, lived with Jim and Abbie part of each year. She received a small Civil War widow's pension and with this money they hired a neighbor girl to help out with the household chores. With this beneficence, Nancy Jane considered it her privilege to run the household and boss everyone around. Abbie and Jim moved upstairs to sleep when Grandma Glore came to stay because there was only one bedroom on the ground floor.

When Granddad Lewis died suddenly one morning in February, 1943, Grandma's life was torn apart. She started dividing her time between the homes of her children, all the while planning to move back to her country home when her bachelor son, Lee, retired from the Great Northern Railroad in Montana and could come home to stay. They would live there together. In the meantime, she would live at the homes of her other children, mostly Aunt Ruth's in Michigan, Aunt Zelma's in Doniphan, and our house. I remember spending one summer with her at her farmhouse when I was thirteen. It was the end of World War II and the first atomic bomb was dropped on Hiroshima while I was there, August 6, 1945. I remember listening to the news on the radio and wondering what in the world it was all about, trying unsuccessfully to understand the report of a bomb of such deadly power.

After we moved to California, Grandma lived with us most of the time. Mom worked and she asked Grandma to start supper for us, which gave Grandma some dignity, feeling that she was needed. Since bedroom space was limited, I slept with Grandma in the same bed and when she got up at night to use the bathroom, it was understood that I would make sure Grandma didn't fall and hurt herself. I styled her hair, fixed her makeup, put on her earrings and generally treated her as a pet. I adored her.

When Uncle Lee died of leukemia before he was ready to retire, Grandma realized that she would never be able to stay at home in her farmhouse in Missouri again. She never complained about the realization that her dream to go "home" would never come to be; it was just a fact that would have to be lived with. She made herself useful at our house, as much as possible, helping out with washing dishes or other simple chores. But if there was any place to go to, she would go and get her purse, putting the handles carefully up on her forearm and modestly saying, "Well, I guess I'd better not go," but in reality waiting for an invitation. She was a little hard of hearing and sometimes got the names of things or places somewhat wrong. Once, when her daughter Ruth scolded her about the danger of traveling with my Dad and Mom in their little Volkswagen retorted, "Well I guess I will ride in that goat wagon if I want to." For a time her favorite television program was "Space Patrol" which she mispronounced "State Patrol." On another occasion, after completing a flight from St. Louis to Los Angeles after she was eighty years old, she told Mom: "I was having a good time on the airplane until they put some old woman in the seat next to me." She loved to travel and once said that if she had lived in pioneer times she would have gladly walked across the plains to the west for the sake of the adventure.

While living with Mom and Dad in Riverside, she came down with leukemia and died there in 1958 at the age of 87. She is buried in the cemetery at Big Barren Baptist Church, Ripley County, Missouri.

Living so close to my maternal grandparents was a special gift to me. Because of that, I believe I learned a valuable life-lesson which is love and respect for the older generation.

THE JACKSON FAMILY

JOHN JACKSON, JOHN PENTECOST JACKSON AND WILLIAM P. JACKSON

JOHN JACKSON: Our first proven ancestor in the Jackson family is John Jackson who was born around 1745 in Middlesex Parish, Virginia. He married Elizabeth Bass on July 9, 1769. Their children were:

> **John Pentacost ca 1761**
> William born ca 1770

Their sons were born in Virginia but died in Kentucky which makes me suspect that they must have been in a group of people including our Glore family who moved from Virginia to Kentucky to continue working in the mines.

JOHN PENTACOST JACKSON: This John married Mary Smith on Mach 22, 1783 and they had the following children:

> John L., ca 1784
> **William P., ca 1790**

WILLIAM P. JACKSON, born in Kentucky, died in Washington County, Missouri after 1860. He first married Jinney Salley. Their children were:

> Phillip 1810
> **Smith 1814**
> Andrew "General" 1827
> Frances Minet 1830
> Levitha "Visey" 1846
> Eliza 1850

SMITH JACKSON:

My great-great grandfather, Smith, was named for his maternal grandmother, Mary Smith. He is buried on the family farm on Mineral

Fork River, Missouri, in "little Germany." During a Yellow Fever epidemic, a neighbor died of the disease. Smith gave his only white shirt to the neighbor's family to bury their dead. The very next week Smith died of the same disease and his family had to go to town and get a white shirt for Smith to be buried in. He was thirty-nine years old. Recently the present owner of the farm dug up this grave, thinking it was an Indian grave. He found Smith's skeleton still dressed in the white shirt.

Smith married Susan Horine when she was fifteen years old. Their family:

> Napoleon Bonaparte (Bony) 1838
> Thomas 1839
> **Nancy Jane, January 4, 1842**
> Andrew 1845
> Eliza 1847
> Minerva 1848
> Mary 1850
> Catherine (Kit) 1851
> Elias "Bud" 1853

NANCY JANE JACKSON:

To say that Nancy Jane was a strong woman would be an understatement. She was known to have strong opinions about how everyone in her community should conduct themselves. For instance she let it be known, "No work on Sunday." If she heard about anyone offending this rule, she would summon them and say, "Sew on Sunday, take it out on Monday."

She claimed that she was related to Stonewall Jackson. Her greatest compliment to any family member was, "You've got Jackson blood." Recent research has proven her wrong, but in previous years we fervently believed it and to be complimented in this way was coveted by all.

After Granddad Glore died in 1931, she gave up housekeeping and spent her remaining years at the homes of her children. I remember her staying with Granddad and Grandma Lewis. She ruled the household— no contest. She sat most of the time in the dining room where she could look out the window but also keep her eye on the hired girl. She expected her breakfast at a certain time, a glass of water at 10:00 A.M., then a walk around the room some for exercise, lunch at twelve noon, etc. I remember her walking around the pot bellied stove in the living room and lamenting, "Oh I just don't know why the Lord don't take me." She had a small Civil War widow's pension and with that paid a neighbor girl to come and work for three dollars a week. She kept her eye on that girl and wouldn't allow any dillydallying.

She died at one hundred years of age in 1942. She had seen the country torn apart in the Civil War, had seen the advent of the automobile and the airplane.

Bibliography

Baker, Russell, *Growing Up*, Signet Books, *New York, 1984*

Bonhoeffer, Dietrich, *Letters and Papers From Prison*, Touchstone, updated edition, 1997.

Bragg, Rick, *All Over But the Shoutin'*, Vintage Books, *New York, 1998*

Feiler, Bruce, *Walking the Bible*, Harper Perennial, 2005

Fischer, David Hackett, *Albion's Seed*, Oxford University Press, New York 1989

Grace, Doris J., *Grace, Richard Cookston Grace, Life, Family, and History*, Lincoln, Nebraska, iUniverse, 2006

Hessler, Peter, *River Town: Two Years on the Yangtze*, Harper Collins, New York, 2001

Huddle, William Peter, *History of the Hebron Lutheran Church*, Orange County Review, Virginia, 1990

Manchester, William, *A World Lit Only By Fire*, Boston, Little Brown & Company, 1992

Ponder, Jerry, *The History of Ripley County Missouri, 1987*

Spence, W. Jerome D and David L. Spence, *A History of Hickman County Tennessee*, Gospel Advocate Publishing Co., 1900

Steven, Hugh, *The Nature of Story and Creativity, 2005*

Thurston, Dawn and Morris, *Breathe Life Into Your Life Story,* Salt Lake City, Signature Books, 2007

Webb, James, *Born Fighting,* Random House, Inc., 2004

Worden, Sylvia, Editor, *Voices of the Golden West,* Trafford Publishing, 2008

Zinsser, William, *Writing About Your Life,* Marlowe & Company, New York, 2004